HOW TO *ACCIDENTALLY* SUMMON A DEMON

Scarlett Philips

Written by: Scarlett Philips
Cover Artist: Eve Graphic Design
Formatted by: The Nutty Formatter

This book is dedicated to anyone who has accidentally stumbled upon the best thing in their life. Like Maddy, I found love when I wasn't looking for it. That's normally when the best things happen. When you least expect them.

ONE

MADELYNE

You know the best way to spend your Saturday night? At home, alone, with your cat and a sexy book. Seriously, fuck going out drinking and partying with the girls. I am *not* twenty-one anymore, and quite frankly, that shit looks exhausting. Getting dressed up, fixing my hair and make-up, being around *so many people*? No fucking thanks. I'll just get all cozy in my reading nook with a glass of my new favorite drink, Dreamsicle, and the new book I just bought. It's about this girl that accidentally summons a demon and finds out she's a witch. I just started, but I can tell it's going to be a wild ride.

I keep sipping away as I sail through the chapters. Finally, after hours of reading, I put the book down. I have to pee so bad that I might not make it to the bathroom. In my haste to get to the toilet, I trip over my pants. Seems I thought it would be a good idea to try to take them off while walking to the bathroom... you know, save some time. Jesus, how fucking drunk *am* I? Also, ow! I groan as I rub my knee, I'm definitely going to have a bruise tomorrow. I really wish I had carpet now, might have cushioned my fall just a little.

Groaning, I get my fat ass off the ground and hobble the rest of the way down the hall. "Yup. That hurts. Might have to go to the fucking doctor. Just great," I mumble to myself as I sit down to pee. When I'm finished, I wash my hands and limp back to my seat. I make it only a few steps before I think better of it, and head towards the kitchen instead. I deserve a snack after that ordeal.

Digging through my cabinets, I find absolutely nothing I want to eat. I mean, there's food in there. Fucking shelves are full. But I don't *want* any of it. So what do I do now? I start looking in the cabinets again because I'm *sure* something is gonna look good to me this time around. I finally see the crackers that were literally *right* in front of my face every single time I've opened the door. Ignoring the peanut butter on the shelf, I check the fridge for some cheese because cheese is life.

"Yes!" I cheer and do a little dance in my underwear. Damn, it's a good thing no one can see me. They'd probably think I was a lunatic. Definitely not sexy. Oh, well. "Fuck them and their nonexistent asses. I've got vodka and cheese! I don't need them or their judgments." Hmm, maybe I *shouldn't* make another drink if I'm gonna talk to myself out loud all night.

Carrying my cheese and crackers and boozy orange soda back to the room, I set them down on the side table so I can get comfy again. Once I am, I dive right back into the book. I *have* to know how it ends. Hours later, I can hardly keep my eyes open. Ugh, I don't wanna sleep. I wanna finish this book.

"Jesus, if you can hear me, I'd really like to have a big strong protective alpha male to carry me to bed when I read too much and fall asleep with a book. Is that really too much to ask?" Considering a sexy macho man does not magically show up in my living room to cart my ass off to bed, I guess the big guy upstairs thinks it is. Thanks a lot, Big Guy.

I somehow manage to get myself to the bathroom *again,* strip off the rest of my clothes, *and* walk unassisted to my bed. I think I'll celebrate by passing the fuck out, 'cause damn, I'm tired!

I don't know how much I drank last night, but oh my God. Never again. I mean it this time. Groaning, I roll over, smacking the bedside table, blindly searching for my phone. Dear God, please don't let me be late. Margorie will murder me if I don't show up for church. Fuck, why did I think it was a good idea to get drunk on a Saturday? Finally, I skim the edge of my phone with my fingertips. Almost got it! I reach out again, this time closing my hand around the annoying device and pulling it to me.

Two missed calls and ten texts. And I'm not even late yet. Why? Why is Margorie so neurotic? It's really not necessary to call and text repeatedly to 'remind' me. I *know* we have church. We've gone at the same time every Sunday for as long as I can remember. Since it's unwise to ignore her texts, I quickly write back.

Me: Yes, Mother. I know about church. I will be there. I'm not even late. Give me a break.

Mother Dearest: Madelyne Danica. Don't you get that tone with me, young lady!

Oh my God. If only you could actually hear my tone, *Mother.* Trust me, that was a *nice* text.

Me: Sorry, Mother. I'm trying to get dressed. The longer you text me, the longer it takes me to get ready. Then I'll end up late and you'll be the laughingstock of the town. Wouldn't want that, would we? Gotta go! See ya soon! Xoxo

"Murder is wrong. You don't look good in orange," I chant over and over until I fully talk myself out of sacrificing her during the service today. That and I think my pastor may frown on that kind of thing. Right? Damn, maybe I should pay more attention to what the pastor drones on about every week.

I was somehow smart enough to lay out my dress yesterday, so at least I don't have to take time to find something to wear. Digging through my underwear drawer, I find the lacey white bra that goes with the dress. It has a vee neckline, so I have to be careful which bra I wear with it. After putting it on, I slip the silky maroon dress on, tie the sash on the side, then hurry to the bathroom to finish getting ready. I throw my long brown hair up in a messy bun and get to work on my face. I've always had naturally flawless skin, so I don't like using a lot of product, but I love doing my eyes. My favorite silver eyeliner and gray eyeshadow really make my brown eyes pop. Just as I'm finishing up, my phone rings. Rolling my eyes, I pick it up, stopping short when I see the name. *Dad.*

"Hi, Dad!"

"Madelyne," my hero grumbles down the line.

"What, Dad? I'm not even late!" I defend myself petulantly before he even starts whatever lecture Margorie has convinced him to give me.

"Yes, well. You know Margorie doesn't like being tardy, and you are *always* late. For some reason, she thinks if she constantly blows up your phone, you'll just get up and get there on time. So how about you try that? It would save a lot of heartache for a lot of people," he teases. Or at least I hope he's teasing.

"I'm almost ready, Dad. I was just putting on my make-up before I left." I don't know what her fucking problem is. She's my fucking *stepmother*. She has no right to dictate my life the way she tries to all the damn time.

"You know you don't need any of that crap. You're beautiful just the way you are. Now, put the make-up down and get to the church before we do, okay?"

"You haven't even left the house? Then why is she yelling at me already?" Ugh, the woman is so overbearing, I swear.

"Madelyne," he snaps. "What did I tell you?"

"I know, I know. I'm coming. I'll be there before you… if you take your time. Love you, Dad! See you soon." I rush the last bit out and quickly hang up before he can yell at me.

I pull up to the tiny church my dad and the wicked witch of the west go to, the same one they have been dragging me to since I was a kid. I didn't have a choice when I was a child, but you'd think at twenty-five, I would be considered *grown* and could make decisions for myself for a change. Guess I was wrong. *Mother Dearest* somehow always gets her way. I keep telling myself to take a stand. Tell her I don't believe in God. That if demons were real, they'd probably be really good in bed. Okay, maybe I wouldn't tell her *that*. But I need to tell her something. This whole going to church thing is eating into my valuable reading time.

Getting out of my car, I make my way to the lobby to wait for the parentals. Have I mentioned how much I dislike Sundays? I call it torture Maddy day. Has a nice ring to it, doesn't it?

"Oh, Maddy. So good to see you." Tiffany chitters, flipping her long blonde hair over her shoulder as she stops in front of me on her way inside the sanctuary.

God, I hate when she does that, calls me Maddy like we're friends. Her dad's some bigshot politician or something and he wants her to follow in his footsteps, starting with law school. My dad owns the biggest law firm in town. For some reason, she thinks she can cozy up to me to land a coveted internship. Too bad for her, if I had any say in it, I'd make sure she flunks out of college. She's a self-entitled bitch. She doesn't deserve to work anywhere near my dad.

"Tiffany." I prattle back with a huge plastic smile. "I swore I just saw you yesterday. Or was it Friday? The days are just so busy." I'm certain she can hear the disdain dripping off my voice.

That fact is clear when she responds by sneering at me, then turning and storming off. Thank God. I don't know how much more of that I could take. Tapping my toes impatiently, I look around for Margorie, finally spotting her walking toward the entrance, only pausing to talk to the greeter. I wave as I see her.

"See, not late." I smile brightly. Maybe a little too brightly if her judgy look is anything to go by.

"Yes, a true miracle," she retorts snidely. She's perfectly put together, as always, but no matter how pretty she is, there's just something ugly about her. It's like her vile soul is trying to show itself.

"Now, now, you two. Let's get inside before Pastor Bobby starts," my dad magnanimously cuts in before Mother Dearest can say anything else.

Just another reason I love that man so much. I don't know why he puts up with her shit, but at least he tries to protect me from it as much as he can. I throw my arms around his waist and lie my head on his shoulder. I'm pretty tall for a girl and he's about average in height, so with my heels, we're about nose and nose. Looking at the two of us together, you wouldn't believe we're related. Dad always says I look just like my mother, and based on the fact he's pole thin with sandy brown hair and I'm thick and curvy with hair so dark it could be black, I'm inclined to agree.

"Hi, Dad. How was golf yesterday?" I ask, genuinely curious as we walk into the sanctuary and find seats.

"Golf was fine. Chad asked about you again." He raises one brow and smirks. I just glare at him in return, causing him to let out a deep rumbly laugh that echoes through the room, much to Margorie's horror. "Alright,

alright, I'll leave it alone," he chuckles, raising his hands in surrender. "But you know that boy is crazy about you. Don't look at me that way. I'm just stating the obvious."

"Well, why don't you state the obvious that he's a complete moron. You know he couldn't handle a woman like me, Dad. He'd try to change me in some way, then I'd have to crush him like a bug."

Mother Dearest scowls while Dad just shrugs his shoulders and nods in agreement. He knows. Margorie, of course, thinks we'd make a perfect couple, but she doesn't know anything about me. The real me. She doesn't *want* to know. As long as I play along and pretend to be the perfect daughter, she couldn't care less.

All conversation comes to an end as Pastor Bobby begins his speech about whatever bible story he's come up with this week. Something about how we should all repent so we don't go to Hell. I zone out because I don't really care, and I'd rather think about the book that's waiting for me when I get home. Margorie would have a conniption if she knew I was reading about witches and demons, let alone fantasizing about a demon doing to me what the demon does to the girl in the book. Don't even care if it's a one-way ticket to Hell. What a way to go!

TWO

BELZAR

I have no idea how I was summoned, but I decide to stay hidden until I know what the fuck is going on. My friends have all been summoned at some point, but I *never* have. Yet, somehow, here I am standing in front of a beautiful woman, mesmerized by her curves. She's wearing a form-fitting shirt that may cover her entire upper half but leaves nothing to the imagination. I can see exactly how big her tits are, too big to fit in my large hands, and her soft belly, that I want to caress, to know if the skin is as silky as I imagine. Her pants are tight, hugging her legs, accentuating her curves. I want to know everything about this woman.

I watch as she walks from her kitchen to her living room and sits in a comfortable-looking chair. She sets her drink down on the table next to her and picks up a book instead. As she reads, I lean in to get a look at the book. No idea what it's about, but based on the cover, I'd say some kind of romance book. She mumbles to herself as she reads. It's kind of endearing.

After a while, she places the book on the table beside her, and I back up just in time for her to stand. I watch as she fumbles her way to the bathroom while simultaneously removing her pants, resulting in her tripping over said pants and falling ungracefully to the hard floor. I was already drooling over her ass before she started to peel the offending garment from her body. When she pulled them down to reveal her lacy boyshort panties, I was about ready to show myself. Then she tripped, fell, and hurt herself, and I didn't think she would be too happy to see me. I can't make myself leave though. I want to study this woman. She intrigues me, and I'm not easily intrigued.

Waiting for her to come back, I pick up the book and read the back to see what it's about. I'm shocked to find it has a demon in it. Is that the kind of thing she's into? Is that why she summoned me? She wants to see if demons are anything like in the books?

She finally comes out of the bathroom but stops in the kitchen. I hope she's getting something to eat. I'm pretty sure she's had enough alcohol. Walking to the kitchen, I hear her cheering something about cheese. I turn the corner to see her dancing half-naked in her kitchen. She's so fucking gorgeous, I want to bend her over that counter and show her real demons are *better* than the books. She mumbles something about not needing someone and their judgemental ass, I don't know. She's an interesting human.

That chair must be awfully comfortable because the longer she sits there reading, the more often her eyes slide closed. Every time, she snaps them back open, shakes her head, and goes right back to reading. I'm going to have to read this book, see what has her staying up when she's obviously exhausted. Finally, she realizes maybe she should go to bed. This decision is vocalized by her asking Jesus for a big strong man to carry her off to bed. Once again, I almost reveal myself. I would be more than happy to take this temptress to bed. When no such man appears in front of her, she sighs and drags herself to bed, managing not to fall this time.

I follow her to her room, just to make sure she gets there okay, not to be creepy or anything. Ripping off her remaining clothes, leaving her bare for my eyes to devour, she then throws herself on the bed and instantly passes out, her soft snores filling the room. Standing in a corner, I watch her sleep, hypnotized by her steady breathing, watching her naked back rise and fall as she sleeps peacefully. Deciding I've probably stayed long enough perving on her delectable ass, I make my way home, wishing with everything in me that she'll summon me again.

Waking up the next morning, I'm assaulted by our hellhound puppy. Whoever opened my door for him to attack me, will pay dearly. Everyone knows, as much as I love Fireball, I can't handle his level of puppy excitement first thing in the morning.

"Who let you in? I think you should go get them. Let them take you for your morning walk. How's that sound, Fireball?" I tell the hound sternly. He barks once then runs out of the room looking for his ticket out of here.

"Belz! What's taking you so long? Come on, we wanna hear about last night! Where the fuck *were* you?" Zarreth calls from down the hall.

I run my fingers through my hair, scratching at one of my right horns. I really don't want to tell those fuckers anything about my night, but I know they'll drag it out of me somehow, so I might as well get over it. Sighing to myself, I trudge down the hall to find my best friends and asshole roommates waiting for me in the kitchen.

"Whoa, you look like shit. Didn't get any sleep? Up late defiling the innocent?" Oz smirks at me. The fucker looks like he's been up for hours and is just dying to get to work, meting out some punishment. He's tall, even more so than me, and intimidating as fuck, to people who don't know him at least. His long brown hair is pulled back and a set of long curving horns sticks out of his head.

I want to punch him in his too handsome face, but I know that won't solve anything. Plus, he likes that kind of thing and I don't wanna start shit today. Maybe tomorrow when I don't have this entrancing girl on my mind. Ignoring him, I make a cup of coffee. I need caffeine to deal with the inquisition that's coming my way. They somehow manage to wait until I sit down with my cup and take a sip of liquid life. I don't know how those humans came up with this, but I'm so glad we can get it down here. It would be torture to not have my coffee.

"Okay, we've waited long enough. Spill. What the fuck happened last night? You just disappeared! Were you summoned?! You *never* get summoned," Zephyr hammers me with questions, his short brown hair sticking up between his small pointy horns like he's been running his fingers through it or likely, pulling on it waiting for me to wake up.

"I was. I think it was an accident though. I still have no clue what she did to summon me, but she was definitely not waiting around for a demon to show up," I start to explain.

"What? *She*? Some chick summoned you? Was she hot? Did you do her?" Oz cuts in.

"No asshat. I did not 'do' her. What the fuck man? As I said, I think it was an accident. She didn't even know I was there."

"Then why were you gone all night?" Zar counters with a raised brow. He may look just like Zeph, but their personalities couldn't be more different. He's the serious one, very analytical, whereas Zeph is like a playful puppy.

"Because I wanted to see if I could find out how she summoned me," I snap back.

"And did you?" he argues with his stupid brow raised.

"Of course not," I grumble to a chorus of laughs. These assholes may be my best friends and lovers, but they find it absolutely hilarious that I have no clue how to get summoned.

"Well, maybe she'll summon you again," Zeph offers with an optimistic smile and a shrug. "If I were you, I'd actually *talk* to the woman if she does. Just saying."

"Thanks. We'll see if she even *can* summon me again. With my luck, it was a one-time fluke." I mean, it *was* the first time I've been summoned, so it wouldn't surprise me if it never happened again.

The guys give me pitying looks until I stand up so fast my seat goes flying into the wall behind me. "Thanks for the concern, but I'm gonna head out. See you later," I grumble as I dump my cup into the sink then walk out of the cramped kitchen. As soon as I make my way outside, I stretch my wings and take off. A good flight always clears my head. Let's hope it works this time.

THREE

MADELYNE

I can't believe it's the first day of school for pre-schoolers. Today is such a bitter-sweet day. I was able to meet most of my students and their parents last week, so I have an idea which parents are going to be fine leaving their kids and which ones are going to be anxious to leave their babies with a stranger, many for the first time. The kids never have that problem. They see all the toys I have around the room and run from them to check out all the fun stuff they're going to get to play with today. I talk several moms down and send them on their way, assuring each one that it will be fine and their little ones are safe with me.

One mom doesn't seem so sure about that. She won't take her eyes off of her son as he explores his new class, ignoring all of the other kids. I don't recognize her from meet the teacher day, so I decide I should introduce myself and see if I can help. Walking over, I greet her with a smile.

"Hi. I'm Ms. Parker. You doing okay?" I ask her gently.

"Not really, no. I've never left him with anyone else. Ever. I don't know if I'll be able to do this. He's not used to other kids. I'm just so nervous, I don't know how he's going to handle a school setting. He doesn't talk, so I worry about him more than my daughter." Her voice shakes as she tells me about her son. "I really wanted to come to meet the teacher day but Zach had a meltdown right when it was time to leave. It took all night to get him to calm down. Oh, gosh, where are my manners? I'm Charlotte."

"It's nice to meet you, Charlotte. Would it make you feel better if I gave you updates throughout the day?" I offer, pleased when her eyes light up. "We have this app we can use to share messages and pictures with parents. We can get you set up with it then I can send you messages throughout the day so you know how he's doing. But I promise he's going to be fine."

Of course, she takes me up on the offer, so I spend the next few minutes getting the app set up on her phone and creating a profile for little Zach. She finally leaves, confident that if anything happens she'll be the first to know.

By the time the day is over, I'm ready for a long soak in my tub. The kids were pretty good for their first day, but four-year-olds have *a lot* of energy, and let me tell ya, I can't keep up. I trudge up the steps to my apartment, stopping short when I see the man pacing in the hall outside of my door. He turns around to pace in the opposite direction, *my* direction, stilling when he sees me. Great. Just who I wanted to see after a long day at work.

"Maddy! I've been waiting for you!" Chad smiles, walking towards me with a bouquet of roses.

"Chad. Why are you here?" I don't move closer to my door. If I do, he'll expect me to invite him in, and hell if I'm doing that. I want to know why he's here and get him gone as quickly as possible, preferably before he ruins my night.

"Always straight to the point, Maddy. I love that about you."

Oh, gag. Please don't use the L-word in relation to me. Ever.

"I brought you these." He tries to hand me the flowers again, but I just can't force myself to take them from him.

"I appreciate the thought, Chad, but I can't accept those."

"What? Of course, you can. It's just a little first day of school gift. No big deal, Maddy. They're just flowers." He rushes out, keeping the smile on his face. I haven't managed to piss him off yet. That's good at least.

"Look, Chad, I've had a really long day and I just want

to curl up with a book and pig out on pasta." I stand perfectly still, waiting for him to give in and leave, or lose his calm and collected exterior and attack me. Which Chad will I get tonight?

"One of these days I'm going to break down that wall, Maddy. You *will* be mine. It's just a matter of time." He sneers. With that not so veiled threat, he storms off, dropping the flowers at my feet as he passes me.

I wait until I'm sure he's gone before I finally turn to my door, unlocking it and heading inside, locking it behind me in case he comes back. I drop my keys in the bowl on the table by my door, then head into the kitchen. I need a drink to calm my racing heart. Can't make it too strong though, I do have work tomorrow after all. I mix my new favorite drink, even though I drank too much of this exact concoction just a few days ago and swore it off. I can't help myself, it's just so fucking good.

I start to strip on the way to my bathroom, throwing my shirt on the floor. I stop short when I come face to face with a man... at least I think he's a man... definitely male whatever he is. Also, *not* human. But holy fuck is he *hot*! He's standing in my living room, blocking my way to the hallway that leads to my bathroom. He's not wearing a shirt, probably because of the wings, but it allows me to count the number of ridges up his stomach and chest, so I'm not complaining. Once my eyes are done with their slow perusal of his sculpted front, I get a good look at his handsome face. He has such amazing bone structure, and

I'm really digging the closely trimmed beard that covers it, without taking away from the sharp features. I finally finish my inspection of the mystery man, examining his horns. Two sets of them! The front ones are short and the back ones curl like a ram's.

"Wh-what *are* you?" I stammer. Whether it's from nerves or arousal I'll never tell.

"I believe you know what I am," he responds in a voice that sounds like melted chocolate tastes. I don't even know if that makes sense, but that's how he sounds.

My eyes flick from his double set of horns to his wings, and down further to the tail I hadn't noticed until now. Snapping them back up to his face, I gasp. "You're a d-demon." It's a guess, but I'd say chances are pretty good I hit the nail on the head.

"I am." Is his simple reply.

"Wh-what are you doing here?"

"I was hoping you could tell me that," he tells me smoothly.

"How could I tell you that? It's not like I summoned you or something." I roll my eyes as I put my hands on my hips.

His eyes go black and his nostrils flare as he stares at me and I finally realize I'm standing in front of a *demon* in just my bra and pants, and my hands on my hips are sticking my breasts out like I'm inviting him to have a taste. Which might not be the worst idea I've ever had, but I should probably cover myself. I cross one arm over my chest and the other across my stomach, covering as much as I can. My breasts are far from perky apples, more like cantaloupes, so they're not exactly easy to cover. I'm sure he still has a pretty good view of my cleavage. I'm a big girl, so there's still plenty showing, but what else can I do? The demon before me shakes his head, blinking rapidly as he attempts to focus on something other than my bosom proudly on display.

"You most certainly *did* summon me. It's the only way for me to be here. I can only leave Hell if I'm summoned, and you're the only person who's ever accomplished that feat, and you've done it twice now. I would love to hear how you do it."

What? I not only summoned him, but I've done it *twice*?! "What do you mean, I've summoned you twice? This is the first time I've seen you, and trust me, I would remember." I can't stop myself from checking him out again. Damn, he's a sexy demon.

"Well, I was a little caught off guard the first time. In all my hundreds of years, I'd never been summoned. I wasn't sure what I was walking into, so I remained hidden. This time when you summoned me, I couldn't make myself hide from you. I didn't want to."

"Just how long did you stick around here hidden? When was this?" I'm sure no matter when it was, he saw me do something embarrassing. I do something embarrassing every day.

"It was three days ago. You mostly just sat in that

chair and read. Though you did trip over your pants walking to the bathroom and danced half-naked in the kitchen."

Oh, Jesus Christ! He *saw* that?! My hands cover my face and I whine to myself, utterly embarrassed. Until I feel hot hands on mine, pulling them away from my face. Blinking my eyes open, I'm shocked to see him standing right in front of me, holding my hands between us.

"Please, don't be embarrassed. That's one of the reasons I didn't show myself that night. I didn't want you to be embarrassed that I saw you like that. Besides, the dancing was sexy, enthralling. Definitely not something to be ashamed of."

Well fuck. If he likes it when I dance half-naked, I can do that right now. No, Maddy. No naked dancing for the demon. Behave. Damn it. I hate it when I talk myself out of being bad. I'm always such a good girl. I go to church, I listen to my parents, I teach pre-school, I don't party, I'm not promiscuous. My only guilty pleasure is my dirty romance books, and right now I feel like I'm living in one. He still has a hold of my hands, and I feel like I'm being lulled into submission as he gently rubs the tops with his thumb.

"Is there anything you did tonight that you did on Saturday?"

"I don't know! I just got home. I've been at work all day, and I didn't work Saturday. Honestly, besides reading my new book, I don't even remember what I did." I can tell it's important for him to know how I summoned him, but I just don't know.

"Please? Think hard. What did you do tonight when you got home?"

I recount my night, starting with climbing the stairs to my apartment and finding Chad waiting for me. When I get to the part about Chad, he starts to grind his teeth, and is he growling? Finally, I tell him about me making a drink to erase the experience and his whole face lights up.

"That's it!" He wraps his arms around me and picks me up, spinning me. By the time he stops and puts me back down, we're both laughing.

"What? What'd I miss?" I can't keep the smile off my face. His happiness has taken over me.

"Your drink! You were drinking Saturday too! Was it the same drink?" he asks excitedly.

"Oh! Yes, I tried a new drink Saturday and I really liked it, so I made it again tonight, even though I got a little too drunk the other night and swore I'd never drink again. Dealing with Chad always leads me to drink. But you don't want to know about that. You want to know about the drink. Right! It's called a Dreamsicle. You're supposed to mix orange juice and whipped cream vodka, but I didn't have any OJ, so I used orange soda," I explain.

He cups my cheek and gazes into my eyes. "You're adorable when you ramble. Do you know that?"

I swallow the lump in my throat at his statement. Not that I don't get called adorable, but not normally in relation to my rambling. Most people hate my rambles. His thumb running over my bottom lip pulls me from my inner rambling and back to the here and now, where there's a sexy demon that appears to be flirting with me for some reason.

"Sorry, I was just doing some more of that rambling you adore so much. Thought I'd keep it to myself this time though."

"Don't do that. Why would you deny me the pleasure of listening to your rambles?" His smooth chocolaty voice pours over me and I want to give him anything he asks for. This man is dangerous with a capital D.

"You may think you want all of my rambles, but trust me, you don't. Now, is there anything else I can help you with, mister demon? Because it's time for me to have a long soak in my tiny ass tub."

"It's Belzar, but call me Belz. And you are?"

"Madelyne, but you can call me Maddy. Feel special, it's not a privilege I hand out to just anyone."

He smirks at that. "Well, Maddy, it was wonderful to meet you. I can't wait to see you again. I'll leave you to your relaxing bath. Don't stop making that drink, now. I'm thoroughly enjoying my leave from Hell. You don't even have to drink it if you don't want to. Just mix it every now and then so I can visit, okay?" he implores me and I'm too weak to say no.

Once I agree to continue mixing his drink, he disappears and I head to my bath. What a strange day.

FOUR

BELZAR

Maddy. I can't believe she actually summoned me again. I couldn't hide myself this time. As soon as she summoned me and I popped into her apartment, I was fully visible. She was so distracted she didn't even notice me until she started heading to the bathroom. That entire meeting went a lot better than I expected. Did I expect her to show me her tits and flirt with me? No, absolutely not. Did I expect her to scream like a banshee as soon as she saw me in all my demon glory? Absolutely. I'm sure she was in shock though. There's no way she would have reacted like that if she understood what was going on.

Not that I would ever hurt her, but she doesn't know that. She even agreed to summon me again so I could spend some time out of this hellhole. She's an incredible person just for that promise, and I truly believe she'll keep it. She's also extremely sexy. I had a hard time controlling myself around her. I couldn't even keep my hands to myself. I just *had* to touch her. I know if she keeps summoning me, I'm going to take things further. I hope she's up for that because I don't know how long I can fight this pull that I have to her.

I want to repay her for the reprieve from Hell, no matter how short it was. I'm sitting in the living room trying to think of something nice I can do for her when Zeph comes home.

"Hey, Belz. What's up?"

"I got summoned again," I tell him with a huge smile covering my whole face.

"What?! That's awesome! Was it the same chick? Did you figure out how she did it?" he questions as he sits down next to me.

"It was, we did. She even said she'd summon me every now and then just to get me out of Hell for a little bit. Think I'm fallin' in love man."

"Oh, man. Already? I thought you were supposed to be a tough guy? Come on Belz, don't do this. You know you can't leave Hell unless someone summons you. You've been stuck for hundreds of years and someone just accidentally summons you and you get a taste of what it's like to be out of here. That's not love."

"I know that. I'm not stupid," I snap. "You don't know this girl though Zeph. She's something special."

"Whatever you say, babe. Just try not to get your hopes up, okay? Because we're gonna have to be the ones that put you back together when this goes south."

I hate it when he gets all logical and shit. But fuck, he doesn't know. He doesn't know what it's like to not be able to leave. Deciding I need some alone time, I stand and head back to my room, telling Zeph bye on my way out. I don't want his negativity right now. Even if it is realistically what's going to happen. I want to believe that Maddy won't do that. That she'll keep summoning me. I replay our conversation, again and again, I've memorized every detail.

I've got a feeling I'm going to need to keep an eye out for this Chad asshole. He sounds like trouble. I could just get rid of him, but I doubt that would be the way to win her heart. Then I remember her comment about taking a bath in her tiny ass bathtub. She has a standard-size tub/shower combo. Definitely not enough room for a woman to soak after a stressful day. That's what I'll do! I'm certain she'll appreciate that.

I lie back in my bed and picture Maddy's bathroom. Once I have a clear image, I start expanding it, rearranging it. I make it so the bathroom is bigger on the inside, so there's more room while it takes up the same amount of physical space. Next, I reimagine her tub as an extravagant jetted tub with a tray that can float in front of her, holding all of her stuff; her book, her phone, her glass of Dreamsicle. I can't help but smirk at the thought. If she has a Dreamsicle, that means I'll be there. I make the tray so it won't flip over and spill her things in the tub, then move on to her sink. The sink and mirror need to take up the length of the wall. Her cabinets and drawers will always have exactly what she's looking for. When I'm sure I've thought of everything that would make this the perfect bathroom, I mutter 'sic erit'. I feel the wave of power leave me as it rushes to do its assignment. When I'm using this power on something right in front of me, it's pretty much instantaneous, but with it having to travel from Hell to Earth, I have no idea how long it'll take. Hopefully, it's done by the time she gets home from work.

Closing my eyes, I fall into a deep sleep and dream of seeing Maddy again. This time though she doesn't send me away. We take a bath together and I show her how to work the jets.

The next morning I wake up and pointedly ignore the guys as I get ready for work. I leave the house to a roar of laughter. Fuckers. Just wait. One day they'll be the ones telling me they're in love with a woman and I'll be there to rain on their parade.

The flight to work is quick and uneventful. I left early today, so all my fellow demons must still be at home. No one is on the streets yet. There are no booths set up in the town square. It's really quiet and peaceful. Exactly the kind of morning I needed today. I land and walk up to the castle, nodding to the guard as he opens the door.

The castle is pure opulence. With high ceilings, peaked arches, and hallways that go on forever. One of which I stride down, passing portraits of the royal family as I walk with single-minded determination to my destination. Reaching the purple door, I rap twice before opening it. The princess glances up from her book, giving me a weird look.

"You're here awfully early, Belzar. Something you want to talk about?" She arches her brow.

Seeing her sitting there with her dark hair up in a messy bun on her head, reading reminds me of the first time I saw Maddy. I shake my head to clear the thought. I don't need to be thinking about her right now. If I told Zofina about her she'd never leave me alone.

"Nope. Just needed to get away from the guys so I left early. Why? You want me to leave?"

"Don't be ridiculous. I was just curious. So what's on the agenda today? Any threats to look into? Any demons to hunt down?" she asks as she tucks her book between her leg and the seat.

"Don't know, Zo. I just got here." I roll my eyes at her, chuckling when she throws a pillow at me.

I shake my head at her as I walk to my desk. I used to have my own private office but I moved it into her room after… Well, we don't talk about that. Let's just say I work more closely with the princess now.

"Nope! Something's going on. Tell me. What happened? You know I can always tell when you're hiding something from me, you might as well spill it," she argues as she saunters over to me.

"If I tell you, will you leave me alone?"

"Not likely, but you can try," she admits with a bounce of her shoulders and a giggle.

"I may have been summoned the other night," I confess.

"You what?! But you've never been summoned! How the Hell did that happen?" she exclaims.

"No idea, now can we get to work, please? Oh look, there *is* a threat for us to look into. What do you know?"

FIVE

BELZAR

As soon as I walk into the house, I'm wrenched from where I was standing about to pet Fireball, and deposited in Maddy's living room yet again. Man, he's gonna be pissed when I get home.

"How have I not noticed that before? Do you always come in with a cloud of smoke?" Maddy asks as soon as the air clears and she can see me again.

"Most of the time, yes. I can control it if I want to. For example, the first night you summoned me, I stayed hidden because I'd never been summoned before and I wanted to see what was going on before I revealed myself. I must say, I wasn't expecting you to summon me again so soon."

"Oh? You weren't expecting this? It's *such* a surprise?"

She furrows her brows, giving me a look like she isn't buying my shit. "Well, *I* wasn't expecting my bathroom to be changed when I got home from work today. Do you know anything about that?" She has her arms crossed across her ample bosoms and the glare she's giving me is sending mixed messages. She doesn't *look* mad, yet she's trying to act like she is. I swear I will never understand women.

"Of course, I do. Do you like it? I wanted to thank you for giving me the opportunity to leave Hell. It's been torture not being able to leave while seeing my friends get summoned," I admit my deepest pain to the entrancing stranger.

"Oh, Belz, I'm so sorry. I love my bathroom, thank you so much! I have no idea how you did it, and it'll be really hard to explain if I ever have visitors." She gushes while chuckling. "But it's amazing and I can't wait to try out that tub!"

"I can make it so it's your normal bathroom if anyone but you enters," I offer with a shrug.

Her eyes bug out and she shouts, "You can *do* that?! That's amazing! You have to show me!"

I laugh and shake my head at her excitement. "Have you already drank that Dreamsicle? You're all over the place tonight." I can't hide the smile on my face. I love seeing the different facets of her personality.

"Sadly, no. I've got work tomorrow and I learned my lesson from last time. I did *not* want to wake up this morning. Not that I'm usually much of a morning person, but still, I can't do that again. Not so soon anyway," she rambles.

"How *was* your day? Did that asshole show up again? Cause any problems for you?" I ask seriously. I hate the shift in mood when I bring him up, but I want to know if he's causing problems for her. I'll take care of him if he is, and if *I* can't, one of the guys will.

"No," she sighs. "Please don't worry about Chad, he's a menace but I don't think he'd do anything too stupid. For some reason, he has it in his head that I'm going to marry him. Even though we've never even been on a date. I barely talk to the man when I'm forced to endure his company, so I have no idea where he got that thought from. Probably *Margorie*," she sneers the name.

"Who's that? What say does *she* have in who you marry?" I demand.

"Ugh. She's my stepmother. She wants me to do a lot of things I have no interest in doing, but enough about that." She waves the topic off. "I wanna see you work your magic. What kind of powers do you have?" She lights up at the mention of powers and I can see her vibrating with excitement.

Apparently, she's not playing around because she grabs my hand and drags me down the hall to the bathroom. "Show me," she demands, throwing her hand out in front of her without letting go of mine with her other.

"Are you sure you're ready for that?" I smirk down at her.

She just raises a brow in challenge and I shrug a shoulder. Can't say I didn't warn her. Looking into the massive bathroom I designed for her, I imagine it back the way it used to be. Once the image is clear in my mind, I mumble the incantation then watch her face as the bathroom changes before her eyes.

A fire blazes from floor to ceiling, slowly turning to ash as the fire spreads across the room. Once the fire is completely extinguished and the entire room is ash, a magical gust of wind clears the ash to reveal the original bathroom. Maddy's face is quite comical, mouth hanging open, eyes as round as saucers, and her grip on my hand tightens to the point it would have broken if I was human.

"Holy shit, I can't believe that just happened. Oh my God, that's amazing!" she shouts in excitement. The wonder is clear in her voice and I have a feeling she's going to have me showing off this skill frequently.

"Why don't you go in and see which bathroom you walk into?" I tease, loving when her eyes light up at the possibility.

She lets go of my hand, much to my dismay, and walks in, spinning around with her arms spread wide and a smile to match. Seeing her delight at my handiwork brings a pride the likes of which I've never felt before. As a demon, pride is a feeling I'm all too familiar with but never have I felt it to this extent.

"You did it!" she cheers as she runs across the tiny to me, large to her, bathroom, throwing herself at me as she reaches the door where I'm still standing.

Catching her, I hold her tight, not wanting to let go. "You're very easy to please, Maddy," I whisper in her ear, not wanting to break the spell.

"Not really, most people don't care enough to do little things to make people happy. Not that *this* is little, but to you, with your powers, I imagine it was. Thank you, Belz," she whispers back into my ear, running her fingers through the hair at my neck.

I hate that she feels that way. That people don't go out of their way to make her happy, let alone do insignificant things just to bring a smile to her beautiful face. Well, she will never feel that way again. Not as long as I can help it.

She finally starts to pull away from me, and I let her. I don't want to push her too hard. I can wait for her to feel comfortable with me. She surprises me though, she doesn't pull all the way away. Just far enough that she can look at me with her hands still around my neck.

"Do you wanna watch a movie? Have some dinner with me? Do demons eat? Food I mean, like y'all don't eat people or something, right?" she rambles.

I can't help it, I throw my head back and laugh. "No, dear, we don't eat people. And I would love to watch a movie. What kind of movies do you like?"

"Well, how am I supposed to know? You're the first demon I've met." She sticks her tongue out at me and I have a quick vision of her doing something much more enjoyable with it.

Leaning forward, I snap my teeth at the appendage teasingly. She jumps back with a laugh then smacks me in the chest.

"Don't *do* that! You scared me to death. Look, my heart is racing." She takes my hand and places it over her heart.

Must not squeeze her breast. Must not squeeze her breast. I am so focused on the rapid beating and her shaky inhalations, that I notice the second they change, snapping my solid black eyes to her bright hazel ones. The gold is shining in them pulling me in like a beacon, and I see my arousal reflected at me in the brown and green swirls. Her lashes flutter and she licks her lips as we stand there, my hand on her chest, but not as intimately as I would like.

"Have you seen *Little Nicky*?" she breaks the silence, pulling my hand from her breast and all the tension bleeds out of the hall.

"Of course, I have. That's one of my favorite Hell-based movies. I bet you didn't know that it was written by a demon."

"What?! No way!" she cries.

"Oh, yeah. Lucifer's sons weren't too thrilled about it, but Luc thought it was hilarious, so they had to deal with it."

"You're on a first-name basis with the devil?" She pulls me to a stop halfway to the living room.

"Oh, yeah. He's a cool guy. Gets a bad rap but he doesn't let that get to him. Don't believe everything you hear. He's not the evil you should be scared of," I warn her.

"I was actually an atheist until you showed up." She shakes her head with a sigh. "Margorie always forces me to go to church every Sunday, but I mostly tune out whatever the pastor drones on about."

"Well, good. It's mostly all bullshit anyway. Now come on, let's start that movie and you can order some dinner. Don't worry about me, I'll just eat the delivery boy," I tease her with a smirk, earning another smack to my arm as we continue to the couch, making a stop to pick up her phone on the way.

SIX

MADELYNE

I honestly thought I had dreamt the whole thing. When I woke up this morning, I was sure I had made it all up. I mean it's a little far-fetched, right? I accidentally summoned a demon by mixing a drink? That's crazy. But then I got home from another long day of playing with some very energetic kids, only to walk into my bathroom, and feel like I just stepped into a completely different house. There was no explaining it away. My bathroom had magically changed.

It was still the tiny room I've lived with for the past five years since I moved in after graduating college, but once I stepped into the room, it was completely different. Before, I could barely walk around in it. It took two steps to get from the door to the small shower/tub combo and three steps to get to the toilet. But tonight? It was easily five times the size! The tub was bigger than my parent's hot tub and the sink had a long counter that took up the entire back wall, with a mirror to go with it. The toilet was far enough away from the sink I wouldn't hit my elbow on the edge of the counter. The floor was a beautiful blue and grey mosaic tile and the counter was white marble. It was quite literally, my dream bathroom come to life.

After examining the room for longer than it took to realize it was real, I fixed that drink and waited for my demon to show. I was not prepared for the swirling black smoke that filled the room but was utterly amazed when it cleared to reveal Belz. It *wasn't* a dream. Now we're sitting on my couch, watching *Little Nicky* and eating pizza. The delivery boy was spared his life in exchange for the greasy goodness. Kidding, demons don't eat people. They possess them. Though I suppose he should be thankful Belz didn't feel the need to do that. I mean, it would be a massive step down and I would be very sad to not be able to ogle his perfect chest. So maybe *I* should be thankful too.

Since Belz hasn't been topside before, he doesn't know how to retract his wings, so he has to sit on the edge of the couch so there's enough space behind him for them. He tried sitting down normally but it didn't work out very well. He keeps flicking glances at me as he eats his pizza and I keep trying to act like I'm *not* staring at his wings, but I can't help it. You would stare too.

"Maddy." He startles me and I jump like I was just caught with my hand in the cookie jar, which only causes him to laugh that deep rumbly sound I've come to love in such a short amount of time. "You can touch them if you want."

I'm so shocked by his offer, my eyes snap to his. They're a dark brown, like melted chocolate. Right now they look like normal eyes, but I've seen them go completely black before. It's kinda freaky.

"I... I can?" I ask hesitantly.

"Well, I would reach one out to you, but I'm afraid after everything we went through to get them to behave and stay still so I could sit down, they would take it as an invitation to stretch out." He sighs dramatically.

I bite my lip trying to hide my smile. "They really have a mind of their own, don't they?" They were perfectly fine, tucked in behind him, the whole time we were standing talking, but as soon as he tried to sit, they snapped out and took up the entire couch! It was a hilarious sight. Belz was sitting on the far left seat and his right wing flared to cover the length of the couch. I still could have sat in front of it, but he wouldn't have been comfortable. The left wing was bent at a weird angle over the armrest, with the talon-tipped end dragging on the floor. It took forever, but we finally managed to sweet talk them into staying against his back.

"They do. Normally they're more well behaved," he grumbles.

Since I've secretly been dying to touch them, I sit up on my knees and scoot closer to him, carefully reaching one hand out as I do. My fingertips graze along the side of his wing and I watch in fascination as it twitches. The wing's reaction to me bolsters my resolve and I splay my hand wide against it. It feels smooth, almost leathery. Scooting even closer to Belz, I run my hand down the outer edge to where it comes out of his back. He shudders as I trail my fingers along the base of his wing and I start to pull my hand back.

"No. Don't stop. It feels... good. I've never been touched like that before. I like it. You can keep going if you want," Belz groans.

Knowing that it feels good when I touch him like this, I give up all pretenses of not being engrossed and caress them with both hands, carefully listening for any indication that he no longer likes it. What I hear though, is his breathing quickening and low grunts of *pleasure.* Holy shit. Is this turning him on?

"Maddy..." he groans. "You're gonna have to stop, dear. I can't. I haven't. Ooooh."

Yeah, he's definitely turned on. The problem is... I don't want to stop. I want to touch him everywhere. Not just his sensitive wings.

"Belz?"

His head snaps in my direction at my hoarse whisper. His eyes are completely black again. I wonder if they always do that when he's aroused. He must see the question in my eyes because his slowly start to bleed back to normal.

"What is it, Maddy? You can ask me anything."

"What if... what if I don't *want* to stop touching you?" I bite my bottom lip as my eyes widen and I hold my breath waiting for his answer.

"What do you want, Maddy? Whatever it is, the answer's yes. Always. Anything you want that I have to give, I will gladly give it," he declares.

I blink my eyes at his response, clearing the lust fog from my brain, well enough of it, at least. "Is that because I'm the only way you can leave Hell?" I hope he didn't catch the wobbliness in my voice.

I'm surprised when he spins his entire body to face me. "Madelyne, no. That has nothing to do with it. I feel this connection with you. I've been attracted to you since the moment I saw you, but the more I learn about you, the more I want to know. When you threw yourself in my arms earlier, all I could think about was kissing you. I won't lie to you, I'm both thrilled and amazed to be able to spend even a little time away from Hell. But if it were anyone else that could summon me, I would rather stay home. I'm sorry you think that's the only reason I'm here. I could have gone home at any time after you summoned me, but I *want* to stay here, with *you*."

The sincerity in his voice strikes a chord with me. I know deep down, he's telling the truth. He's here because he wants to be, not because he has to be. I hadn't even realized I was worried about that until he just told me. His melted chocolate eyes are pleading with me to believe him, but I already do. To prove it, I lean forward and capture his lips in a kiss, holding the back of his head as I explore his mouth. Seconds later, he wraps both hands around my waist and hauls me onto his lap as he turns so he's facing the TV again.

He runs his hands up my back and I wiggle on his lap, loving the groan the movement pulls from his lips. He nips my lips in retaliation, so I grind myself down on his hardening cock. Oh man, I sure hope he has a normal cock. He wrenches his mouth away from mine and I whine in protest.

"Are you sure you want this? I can't hold back much longer, Maddy. I want you so badly, I burn for you."

"I want it. Please," I pant. "Take me to my bed."

"With pleasure," he growls, standing and carrying me to my room. I don't even care that he already knows where he's going, I just wrap my legs around his waist and cling to him, as I continue to kiss him everywhere I can reach.

Once we're in my room, he strides over to the foot of my bed and tosses me in the middle. I bounce once, twice, before he grabs me by my ankles and pulls me to the edge, where he unbuttons my pants and smoothly pulls them down my legs, throwing them in the corner of the room. He slowly slides his hands up my legs, causing goosebumps to erupt in his wake. I catch his smirk as he bends his head, following his hands with his lips. This time

I shiver as he kisses his way up. His hands grip the waistband of my panties and I silently thank God I wore a cute pair today. He runs his nose over my center before leisurely dragging my panties down, revealing my trimmed pussy to his starving eyes. I'm so empty and needy, but he just strips me of my underwear not touching me where I want, prolonging my torture.

"Belz, pleeease," I whine. I don't know how much of this I can take.

"I've got you, baby. Don't worry," he promises.

But I am worried. I'm worried because I've never felt this before. I've never been this desperate to have someone inside me, to connect with me. He's going to destroy me, I can feel it now. I gasp as his lips return to my flushed skin, skimming up my stomach as he slips my shirt up and off my head, tossing it to join the pile.

"I've been fantasizing about these fucking tits since I first saw you," he groans as he pulls the top of my bra to the side to reveal more of said tit. Then he attacks. Ravishing my breasts, squeezing them in his hands as he kisses, nips, and sucks everywhere he can reach before he finally gets too impatient to have me bared to him and *rips* it off of me.

Seriously, I've read that in books and it just never seemed realistic to me. But I guess a demon would be stronger than the average man and would clearly have no problem ripping my beloved bra to shreds. I'll have to worry about the fact that I've lost my favorite bra later though because holy fuck this demon can suck!

My hands fly to his head, intending to hold him to me as he pulls my nipple into his mouth, but as I'm running my fingers through his long black hair, I bump against his horns. My hands change direction all on their own, I swear I didn't tell them to give up on the hair pulling, but they have other things in mind. Like seeing if those horns are as sensitive as his wings are. I circle my hand around his front horn, stroking it like I would his cock.

"Uuuuugh, fuck, Maddy," he groans and I have my answer.

"What's it feel like when I rub your horn, Belz?" I purr.

"Fucking Devil, you vixen! You know damn well what you're doing to me," he grumbles.

"Now, now. That's not an answer, little demon," I tease, removing my hand from his horn.

That gets the reaction I was looking for because he jerks his head up and glares at me with his solid black eyes. "It feels like you have your hand wrapped around my *cock*. Now, don't tease me unless you want me to tease you," he threatens, and I have no doubt he would follow through, but I've been teased enough for one day.

Leaning over me, he holds himself up with both hands on either side of my shoulders, his wings spread out behind him. He's so fucking gorgeous, I don't know where to look or touch. I settle for cupping his face, smoothing my thumb over his bottom lip.

"You're going to ruin me, I already know it. So why don't you get to it? Show me what a demon can do."

"I'll gladly ruin you, again and again, *Amica Mea.*"

No idea what he called me, but he seals the vow with a kiss so consuming I'm seeing stars by the time he releases me. Leaning on one elbow, he glides his other hand down my side, across my pelvis, and finally to my dripping entrance. He slips his finger through my folds, collecting my moisture then circles my clit with his wet digit. I buck my hips and moan in response.

"Please, Belz. I need you. No more teasing."

"No more teasing, *Amica Mea.*" He proves he means it by pushing his finger into my tight hole.

"Ooooh, yes. More. Please." I cry at the welcome intrusion.

His finger twists inside me and soon he's adding a second and a third, stretching me so good it aches. As I'm writhing on the bed from his fingers, he dives down and begins to lavish attention on my abandoned breasts, nipping and sucking on my nipples. That puts his horns right in my face and I decide if I can't reach his cock, I'll just do what I want to do to it to his horns. So I wrap my hands around the front two horns, stroking up and down as I lean forward to lick the tips one at a time. Of course, me playing with his horns makes him double down on his ministrations. I cry out when he finds my g-spot and just keeps rubbing it, faster and faster until I gush all over his hand.

He pulls away from me and I watch in awe as he brings his dripping hand to his mouth and licks my cum off, sucking on his fingers until they're clean. Holy fuck that was hot.

"I think you might be ready for me now, beautiful," he declares as he stands up and starts to strip his pants off of his muscled legs.

SEVEN

BELZAR

She tastes like fucking ambrosia and her moans are my new reason for living. I can't believe she made me come in my fucking pants. I was not prepared for her to suddenly start stroking two of my horns at the same time. Then she had to go and lick their tips. I couldn't control myself. I don't know how long it's been since one of the guys has played with my horns, but fucking hell, it felt good.

I strip off the offending pants, pleased to find my cock is already rock hard again and ready for action. I pump it once, then twice, watching Maddy as she inspects me in all my naked glory. Her eyes are wide as they're locked on my erection and I'm starting to worry about what's going through her head right now.

"Holy shit, what is *that*?" she exclaims, before crawling to the edge of the bed and hesitantly wrapping her hand around my cock. "Oh my God, it has ridges. Brings a whole new meaning to *ribbed for her pleasure*."

She continues to inspect my cock, stroking her hand up and down, testing my resolve. "You have a fancy peen! Do all demons have fancy dicks?" She looks at me through her lashes as she continues to play with my dick and I can't take it.

"There will be no talk of other penises while you're holding mine. Now, how about I show you how much pleasure my *fancy peen* can give you?"

Her eyes flare and she bites her lip, flicking her eyes from mine to my cock still in her hands, and back again. Finally, she smiles the most seductive grin and slowly nods. Letting go of my cock, she sinuously moves back up the bed.

Chasing after her, I push her back so she's laying down again, then spread her legs as I crawl between them, the head of my cock bumping against her sensitive clit and I chuckle as she groans.

"I got you, baby, don't worry. I'll take care of you," I promise her, meaning every word far more than she thinks. I'm not just talking about here and now. No. Now that I've had a taste of her, she's mine. She just doesn't know it yet.

Grabbing my cock, I rub it through her folds collecting her cream as lubricant. Finally, I start to slowly push in, cognizant of every whine and whimper falling from her lips. I know I'm big and she's never had anyone like me before. To help ease the sting of my intrusion, I rub circles around her clit and lean down to suck her nipple again. I can't get enough of her fucking tits. I love the way the hard bud feels in my mouth as I roll my tongue around it. She starts groaning and her pussy gets wetter and wetter, easing my way. I want her to enjoy this so I start doing easy shallow thrusts until she wraps her legs around my waist and bucks her hips up to meet me.

"Oh, Jesus Christ, Belz! I'm *fine*! Just fuck me!" she cries.

I can't help the laugh that falls from my lips. I swear this woman is something else. "You know, I don't think he would like you using his name like that while you're getting railed by a demon, *Amica Mea*."

"Why don't you start railing me and we'll find out." She raises her brow in challenge.

"You know I love your sass, Maddy. If you wanted more, all you had to do was ask," I inform her then buck my hips, slamming all the way home. And fucking Hell. She's tight.

We both let out matching groans and I slowly pull out, just to thrust back in.

"Holy fuck. I'm a big fan of the ribbed cock. Huge. Oh, God," she moans.

"That's right, baby. Once you go ribbed you never go back." I wink at her and we both crack up laughing at my lame joke, her pussy squeezing me so tight I can't take anymore.

Over and over I pound into her until she screams my name. Spent for the moment, I collapse beside her, one of my wings covering her and the other hanging off the bed. We lie there panting, trying to catch our breaths after that mind-blowing orgasm.

"Well, I'm officially going to Hell, aren't I?" she murmurs.

Scared I made a mistake, that she didn't want this, I raise my head so I can see her face. "Do you regret it?" I ask.

She rolls over to face me and I'm struck by the love in her expression. She's not mad at all.

"Of course not. I could never regret you, Belzar," she tells me, as her smile stretches across her face.

She looks like she wants to say more, but I don't give her the chance. I surge toward her and claim her lips. I have never kissed anyone with so much love, so much passion, and she matches me every step of the way. Showing me with her tongue battling mine that I'm not alone in this. My feelings aren't one-sided. I end the kiss, pulling back to gaze into her warm eyes.

"You're mine now, Madelyne. I'll never leave you. I'll spend the rest of eternity making sure you feel loved and cherished." She may think they're just pretty words, but they're my solemn vow. One I can't break even if I wanted to.

Her smile leads me to believe she just might understand what really happened and she looks to be okay with it. She cups my cheek, brushing her thumb across it as she stares into my bottomless eyes.

"I love you too, Belzar. You're worth going to Hell for. Besides, I'll have you when I get there, right?"

"Absolutely, *Amica Mea*. Nothing could keep us apart."

"Good. When do you have to go back? Can you stay and hold me? At least until I fall asleep?"

"I can stay as long as you want me." I kiss her forehead and tuck my wings in so I can lie down next to her. "Come here," I command with my arm open for her.

She wiggles next to me for a moment until she gets comfortable and lays her head on my chest, placing her arm over my waist.

"I'll always want you, Belz. You're always welcome in my home. Even if I don't summon you," she says around a yawn. It's not long before she's softly snoring away on my chest.

I wake up after the best night's sleep of my life and find a head of brown hair covering my chest. I smile as I look down at the woman that changed my whole world with one drink. I wasn't *miserable* in Hell. I had the guys and Fireball, but it was a mundane existence. Now I have something to live for. Something to look forward to every day. I can't help the smile that covers my face as I gently run my fingers through her hair. She starts to stir and I go still. I guess that was the wrong move though because she pops her head up and looks at me with furrowed brows.

"Why'd you stop?" she grumbles.

"My apologies, *Amica Mea*. I didn't want to wake you," I tell her, then gently coax her head back down and resume my ministrations.

"Mmmm well, I need to wake up soon anyway, I have to get ready for work. This is a much nicer way to wake up than my stupid alarm clock though," she says through a yawn.

"My fingers are at your service, my lady," I pledge, only half-joking.

"Yes, and what lovely fingers they are, good sir." She chuckles and I lean down to kiss the top of her head.

"How long before you have to leave, *Amica Mea?* I never did show you how to use your new tub last night."

"Oh, now that's something worth being late over!" She jumps up looking around, for what I don't know. Finding whatever it is, she bends over putting her bare ass in my face and I'm tempted to lean over and bite it. Before I can though, she pops back up with her phone in hand. "I've got an hour before I've gotta leave, so it'll have to be a fast *bath* but I'm sure we can manage," she tells me with a smirk.

I take that as the challenge it's meant to be and jump

out of bed, wrapping one arm around her waist and the other under her knees. Standing with her in my arms, I take off down the hall to the bathroom. Flicking on the light, I stride over to the tub, setting her down on the edge so I can turn the water on. It fills much faster than you would expect of a tub this size. Actually, it probably fills faster than the original tiny tub, because it's full within minutes and I'm helping Maddy step down into the hot water.

Once she's safely in the tub and sitting on the underwater bench, I climb in, telling my wings to behave themselves. Luckily I had them in mind when I made the bath, so there's plenty of room for them to spread out if they chose to ignore me, which is highly likely. I sink down across from her, rolling my eyes when my wings fan out, splashing water. She chuckles at their antics and swims over to me.

"Thank you for my new tub, Belz. I've never had one I could actually cover my entire body in, much less swim across. It looks like your wings like it too." She smirks at me and I flick water at her.

"Come here, let me show you how to work the jets," I offer suggestively.

"I think I know how to work jets, Belz. It's not rocket science ya know." She rolls her pretty eyes at me, but she's floating close enough for me to grab her and pull her into me.

"It's awfully early for all that sass, isn't it?" I playfully nip at her lips then kiss them. "Now, about those jets…"

Reaching behind me, I press the button and the tub quickly fills with bubbles. She's about to say something smart again, but I silence her by standing and spinning us, so I'm behind her and she's facing the bathroom. I guide her so she's kneeling on the bench I just vacated, and push her shoulder blades so she's bent over the side of the tub.

"Ooooh, God!"

"Mmmm, what's that, *Amica Mea*? You don't like the jets?" I reach over like I'm going to turn them off and she grabs my arm stopping me.

"Don't you fucking dare! Uhh. You gonna fuck me now, or am I just gonna use the jets to get off?"

I fist her hair and pull her head, causing her back to arch. "You will do no such thing," I growl. "That is my pussy. Mine to take care of, mine to punish. If you're going to *get off* it'll be with my permission and by my doing. Do you understand, *Amica Mea?"*

"Yes," she hisses.

"That's my good girl," I praise, then slam my mouth against hers, devouring her moans as our tongues battle for dominance. Dominance that is already mine.

Breaking the bruising kiss, I push her back down and rub my aching cock along her folds. As I slide further and further inside her, we both sigh our contentment. She's so fucking perfect for me, I can't believe I found her by chance.

Gripping her hips so tightly she'll have bruises to remember me by, I pound into her, her screams of pleasure filling the room. I take one hand off of her hip to slide it up her chest, then to her throat, gripping it lightly, until she moans her approval.

"That's it, baby. Take my cock like a good girl. Mmmm, you like that jet hitting your clit, don't you, baby?"

"Oh, yes. Yes. Fuck, Belz. Oh, God. Yes! Harder! Fuck me harder!" she chants and who am I to deny her?

I thrust into her over and over, my hips slapping her ass and splashing water all over the place. "That's it, baby. Come for me," I command and like the good girl she is, she comes all over my cock, squeezing me, milking me dry.

Slowly, I pull out of her pulsing pussy, kissing down her spine as I do. I sit on the bench and pull her down on top of me. Running my hand through her hair, brushing it away from her face, I gently pepper kisses all over her as she sags against me.

"Thank you, *Amica Mea.* You did such a good job. I'm so proud of you, baby," I continue to praise her as she snuggles further into my arms, burying her face into my neck.

"God, Belz. What the fuck was that? I've never come so hard in my entire fucking life. It's like your fucking ridges hit every sensitive spot in my pussy," she groans.

I just pet her hair and chuckle. "That was just the

beginning, *Amica Mea.* I'm glad you like my special dick though." I smirk.

She slowly sits up at that. "What does that mean? *Amica Mea?*" she asks with her brows drawn together.

"It means my love," I state simply.

"Am I? Your love?" she asks, nibbling on her bottom lip and looking at me with such hope-filled eyes.

"I wouldn't say it if it weren't true, Madelyne. I've never called anyone else that before, and I never will." It's the absolute truth and I want her to know that without a shadow of a doubt.

She nods with a smile. "Good. I like it."

"Good, because you're stuck with it," I tease her, then kiss the tip of her nose.

She lays her head back down and I hold her, both of us perfectly content in this moment. Until she suddenly sits up, splashing water again, looking around like she's lost something.

"Fuck, fuck! What time is it? I'm gonna be late for work!" she yelps.

Oh. Yeah, I guess I forgot about that. "Calm down, it's okay. We'll get you there on time."

Standing up, I press the button to drain the tub, then help her out and wrap a towel around her. Scooping her back up in my arms, I walk us to her room and set her down on the bed. She turns and grabs her phone, checking the time as I look at her expectantly.

"Oh, thank fuck. I have ten minutes before I have to

leave. I love you, but I have to get ready. I can't be late." She jumps up and runs to her closet while drying herself off.

I dry myself and get dressed while she hides in the closet, presumably getting ready herself. Two minutes later she rushes out of the closet, fully clothed, and takes off back to the bathroom. I sit on the bed, trying to stay out of her way. I may not have much experience with women, but I know that much. Eventually, she comes back to find me.

"Thank you for last night... and this morning." She smiles as she no doubt recalls exactly what she's thanking me for. "Do you want to come back tonight?" She chews on her bottom lip and fidgets with her hands.

"Of course I do, *Amica Mea.* I thought I told you? I always want to be with you. Whenever you want me. You know how to get me." I wink at her, loving the giggle that falls from her lips.

"Okay, then I'll plan on summoning you as soon as I get home. I don't know how time works down there, but I normally get home around six my time. Hopefully, nothing comes up." She wraps her arm around my waist and my arms and wings both wrap themselves around her in return. "I love you, Belz. See you soon."

"I love you too, Madelyne. Have a good day at work."

And with that, she's off, and I have to go back home. I'm sure the guys are going to give me a hard time for being gone so long, but I couldn't help it. I want to spend as long as I can with Maddy. They'd understand if they knew her.

EIGHT

MADELYNE

"**M**addy! I've been looking everywhere for you!"

Ugh. "What do you want, Chad? You know I don't like it when you come to my work like this." Why does he keep showing up? Why won't he just take the hint and leave me the hell alone?

"Well, I *tried* to talk to you at your apartment, but you wouldn't listen." The glare he gives me belies the sweet tone he's using and I have no doubt if we weren't in public right now, I'd be dealing with a whole different Chad.

"And you thought that meant you should accost me at work? I'm not seeing your reasoning, Chad."

"Please. I'm not *accosting* you. I'm picking you up for our date," he informs me with a shark-like smile.

"We don't *have* a date, Chad. I should know because I would *never* agree to go out with you. Why can't you understand that?" I throw my hand up, shaking it as I talk to make my point.

His smile morphs into something more frightening, something deranged. "You misunderstand, *Madelyne*," he sneers my name and a chill runs down my spine. "You are *mine*. Your agreement is unnecessary." His eyes examine my outfit with clear disdain and he frowns as he finds me lacking. "Go home and change. You have exactly an hour before I'll be knocking on your door. Do not keep me waiting," he threatens, then storms off down the hall.

I stand there, holding my breath until he's out of sight. He's never acted that way before. I don't know what's gotten into him, but I don't really want to find out. Gathering my courage, I turn and walk to my car. And run straight into a wall of muscle.

"Oh, God! I'm so sorry! I was distracted, I didn't even see you there!" I apologize profusely.

"No, no, entirely my fault." A low smoky voice rebuts.

I slowly look up and up and up, discreetly examining his body as I find his face, more than a foot above my own. God, he's *tall!* And extremely handsome. He has short brown hair, shaved close on the sides and a little longer on the top. A pretty popular style, but damn can he rock it. His lips are full with a cupid's bow and I want to lick them. Until I snap to my senses and remember Belz. I don't know that we're exactly exclusive, but until we have that talk, I won't be flirting with any god-like men. I finally meet his eyes and at first, I swear they're black, like Belz's, but after blinking a few times they appear to be just a dark brown. *Come on, Maddy, it's not like every guy you meet is going to be a demon.*

"Was that guy bothering you?" he asks cooly.

"Oh, him? No, it's fine. He's a family friend. Nothing to worry about." I don't know why I downplay what just happened, habit I suppose, but I don't know this guy and by the ice in his tone, I can't be sure he wouldn't go after Chad if I said yes.

"Okay… then why, and *how*, did you summon me?" He studies me carefully.

His words finally click and I gasp. "I summoned you? You're… you're a *demon?*" I whisper the last word, not wanting to be overheard.

"I am. Do you summon my kind often?" He raises a brow in question, but he doesn't seem mad, just curious.

Sighing, I shake my head and start walking again, not surprised at all to find him keeping step with me. "You're the second one this week actually. I don't even know how I'm doing it."

"Well, that's an interesting conundrum."

"Why don't you look like a demon? My other… I mean *the* other demon has wings and horns, hell even a tail. You look like a normal, albeit extremely tall and handsome man."

"Oh, he does, does he? Well, your other demon…" he

starts with a smirk. "Is a very bad boy. We're not supposed to appear to humans in our true form."

"Oh. So he can change forms too? So he looks human?" I ask, excited by the prospect.

"Just what does this demon mean to you? Why do you want him to look human?" he questions.

Shit. I'm talking too much. I don't want to get Belz in trouble. "I don't know what you're talking about. I was just curious as you're only the second demon I've encountered. I didn't ask the last one too many questions." I'll have to ask him a whole host of them tonight. "I'm sorry, I have to go. I have someone meeting me at home soon."

"Hopefully not that douche," he grumbles.

"Yeah... hopefully not. Well, thanks for the talk. Bye!" I walk up to my car and open my door, turning to see him still standing where I left him. "Oh. What's your name?" I quickly ask.

"Zephyr. If you ever need me, just call." He winks and disappears.

I break all of the speed limits the entire way home and run up my stairs as fast as I can, hoping and praying Chad's not already waiting for me. I know he said I have an hour, but I wouldn't put it past him to be waiting for me outside my door... again. By the time I get to my floor, I'm huffing and puffing and I feel like I might die. I really need to start exercising more, but I just don't want to. I breathe a sigh of relief when I turn down the hall and see it's completely empty. No Chad in sight. Unlocking my door, I push it open a little too hard and it bangs against the wall. I rush inside, slam the door behind me, and double lock it.

Finally in the kitchen, I summon Belz, chewing my lip and fidgeting while I wait for the smoke to clear. As soon as it does, I wait a beat to make sure it's Belz, then throw myself at him. He manages to catch me and I wrap my legs around his waist as his arms and wings both cover my back.

"I missed you too, *Amica Mea,* but is something wrong?" he whispers the question into my hair as he holds me tight.

Pulling my head back slightly I tell him about Chad's visit and not so veiled threat. I can feel his entire body vibrate with rage as he listens to my story.

"He's coming here?" When I nod, rubbing my face into his neck he growls, "I'll take care of him. Don't worry about a thing, *Amica Mea.* No one threatens you and gets away with it."

He carries me to the couch and gently sets me down. I watch in astonishment as he changes forms. I can tell he's concentrating extremely hard. I don't think he's ever had to do this before. He was annoyed last night that his wings were in the way, but I told him to leave them. I liked looking at them and turns out *he* liked me touching them, so it was a win-win. But seeing them disappear, along with the horns and tail, I'm reminded of Zephyr. Not that they look anything alike, but what are the odds I would accidentally summon *two* demons?

As soon as his transformation is complete and he looks as human as he can while still looking like a sex god, I start to tell him about Zephyr. Unfortunately, as soon as I open my mouth, there's a loud banging at my door. I don't know why I'm nervous, Belz could kill Chad in the blink of an eye, but I can't help it. I despise confrontation. Which when you think about it, explains my relationship with my stepmother.

"Stay here. I'll take care of him," he commands and I don't even attempt to argue. I don't want to leave this seat anyway.

Turning, I watch him walk to the door but lose sight of him once he gets there. It sucks that I can't see, but that means Chad won't be able to see me either. I hear the door open as it sounds like he rips it off its hinges and it slams against the wall again.

"What?" he snarls.

"Who the fuck are you?! Where's Maddy?" Chad snaps back.

"Don't you fucking worry about who I am, and you have no business with *Madelyne*. Only her friends call her Maddy, and *you* are no friend of hers," Belz sneers.

"Listen here asshole, I don't know who you think you are, but *Maddy* is *mine*."

"Really? Because I'm pretty sure she was screaming *my* name last night. Get fucking lost. Don't contact Maddy again, or you'll have me to deal with. And trust me, you don't want that."

Then the door slams and I hear stomping coming in my direction. Belz turns the corner and I'm startled to see him. His entire body is strung tight, and there's murder in his eyes.

"Belz? What's wrong? What happened? Why do you look like you want to kill someone?"

"Because I do," he snaps before he softens his expression and his voice. "I'm sorry, *Amica Mea*. I don't mean to scare you. How long have you known Chad?"

I'm confused by the question but answer hesitantly. "About six months. We met through my parents. Dad owns the best law firm in the area, lots of new lawyers try to get an in with him. He plays golf with him all the time. The first time Marjorie met him, she decided I was going to marry him. Despite my repeated insistence that I was never going to be with him. I suppose he got it in his head that it was already a done deal because Mother Dearest said so. Far be it for me to have any say in my life," I grumble.

I watch as Belz attempts to calm down, taking deep breaths. I'm kind of wondering if I missed something. Maybe something I didn't see or couldn't hear. Something's wrong.

"Chad is a demon, *Amica Mea*. I don't know why he's fixated on you, but I intend to find out."

"A what? He's a *demon*? Jesus Christ, is every guy around me a fucking demon now? Did I somehow accidentally summon him too? Am I some kind of fucking demon magnet?!"

"I don't know, love, but I know a demon when I see one. Especially because he thought he'd try to scare me off by turning his eyes. Obviously, *that* didn't work. What do you mean is every guy around you a demon? I thought I was the only demon in your life," he teases.

Rolling my eyes I retort, "Yeah, well, that was before I started summoning random demons in the middle of my school."

"You what? How did that happen?" He walks around the couch and drops onto it. "Maybe you are a demon magnet." He sighs as he sinks into his seat.

"Well, after Chad harassed me at school, I turned around to walk to my car and ran straight into another demon. I don't know how I summoned him, so don't ask. He was really nice though, walked me to my car, made me feel safe until I could get in and drive home. He said his name was Zephyr. Do you know him?" I'm sure he doesn't know every demon, but maybe he'll know this one.

"Zephyr? You summoned Zephyr?"

"I mean, yeah? It was an accident. I didn't mean to!" I defend myself.

"I know, *Amica Mea.* I'm not mad. Zephyr is my best friend. One of them at least. We actually live together, with his twin and our other friend Oz. If you ended up summoning them too, I still wouldn't be mad. Did you like Zeph?" he asks with a smirk.

"I mean, I didn't see his full demon form, but he was alright." I shrug and we both burst out laughing.

"Now I know you're lying. Even in his *human* form, Zeph is walking temptation. It's okay if you're attracted to him, Maddy. Don't feel bad about something like that," he assures me.

"Are you and he? Together?" I stumble over the question, but I'm too curious to not ask it.

"On occasion. Relationships are different with demons. Not saying all demons are like us, but we don't put restrictions on our love. I love Zeph as I love Zarreth and Oz, and as Zeph loves Oz... when he's not being a prick. But if one or all of us fell in love with a woman, human, or demoness, we would all be okay with it. I know this because I told them about you today. Me loving you doesn't change my love for them, and me loving them doesn't change my love for you."

Holy shit. "But... they're okay with you being with me? How could that work? That kind of relationship is so foreign to me. Humans are much too controlling and possessive for that to work."

"They were thrilled for me, love. Well, Oz not so much, but he's just a moody bastard. Don't worry about him. For the most part, we're not controlling, though we can be possessive, as you saw this morning." He smirks and the reminder of our time in the tub brings an instant flush to my skin and a self-satisfied chuckle falls from his too sexy mouth.

"And what if... what if *I* didn't want you to be with them anymore?"

"Is that what you want, *Amica Mea?* You want me all to yourself?"

"I just want you to be happy, Belzar. Whether that's with them, me, or both." I grab his hand to make sure he understands I mean it.

His response to that is to manhandle me, picking me up and sitting me on his lap, then grabbing a fistful of my hair, and devouring my mouth. Guess talking time is over. I'm okay with that. I'd much rather *show* him how much I love him.

Running my hands through his hair while our tongues twine together, I startle a little when I get to where his horns should be, not used to him being *human*. I don't let it take away from the moment though, scratching his head and grinding down on his lap. He pulls away long enough to whip my shirt over my head, then tilts my head and starts kissing up my neck. He nips and sucks and I'm a moaning, panting mess as I rock back and forth on his cock. Even through his jeans, I can feel the ridged length begging to be inside me. The rough denim scrapes across my clit through my panties and I cry out. I'm really glad I decided to wear a skirt to work today, otherwise, I wouldn't be able to feel as much as I can.

"Belz. Please. Oh, God! Just fuck me!" I'm not

ashamed to beg. You wouldn't catch me doing it for any other man, but I *know* Belz can make me feel things I've never felt before and I want to get to it.

"Mmmm, you're so sexy when you beg for my cock, *Amica Mea.*" He nips at my ear and I whimper when he squeezes my breasts, pinching my nipples through my bra. "You're wearing too many clothes though."

"Belzar! Don't you dare rip my bra. It's the only one I have since you tore up my good one last night!" I scold him.

"I can make you a hundred just like it, *Amica Mea.* Better even. I *need* to get you out of these clothes. I need to feel your skin against mine as I slowly make love to you."

Damn it, there he goes making me melt. Even though I really want to just ride him hard and fast, I suppose I could allow it. While I'm lost in my head, he tears my bra to shreds. How does he *do* that?! Jesus. I thought bras were stronger than that. And now his mouth is around my nipple, pulling me back to the moment.

His hands leave my breasts, gliding up my thighs, pushing my skirt up to my waist. I can't help the moan as his big hands drift to my ass, squeezing each cheek. It's quickly followed by a squeal as he rips my panties in two then pulls the ruined underwear from between my legs. Sitting up on my knees, I fumble with the front of his pants.

"Jesus Christ! What the fuck are you wearing? How do

I get it off? I'm completely naked now and you're still wearing these cock-blocking pants!" I screech.

He chuckles at my hysterics but somehow manages to pull his pants down. I don't know, maybe it's some demon magic or maybe only a demon can take off demon pants. Hell if I know, but they're gone now as evidenced by the exceedingly hard cock that just smacked my pussy when it sprung free of its entrapment.

More than ready to have him inside me, I wrap a hand around his cock, squeezing his ridges as I guide it to my entrance and slowly sink on it. I pant and moan as he fills me and squeezes my hips so hard I know I'll have bruises tomorrow. I love how he can be rough and tender at the same time. Once I'm fully seated on his cock, he wraps his arms around me, holding me to him, allowing me to get accustomed to his size as I bury my face into his neck, groaning at the sweet stretch. Every time is somehow better than the last and soon I'm rocking on him, wanting more.

"Easy, *Amica Mea.* You may be on top, but this time is going to be soft and slow. I *will* take over if you go too fast," he threatens and I'm not sure if I want to test his resolve or not, but I can't help that my bottom lip sticks out when he tells me I can't ride him hard and fast like I want to. "Now, now. Don't pout, beautiful. Savor the moment."

He doesn't give me a choice in the matter, but I wouldn't have it any other way. Being the good girl I am, I leisurely rock my hips rubbing the tip of his cock against my G-spot as I claw at his shoulders.

"Oh, God! Fuck, Belz! Please, please! Mmmm ooooooh," I whimper as my orgasm washes over me like a cool shower.

"That's it, baby. Let me have it. Cum all over my cock," he coaxes me as he takes over fucking me while I have a seizure on his dick.

His words and movements make me come again, squeezing his cock with a vice grip, pulling him over the edge with me. Completely spent, I collapse on top of him gasping for a breath I can't seem to catch. A problem my asshole demon doesn't seem to have, as he's breathing perfectly normal as he rubs his hands up and down my back, calming my entire body.

"Mmmm, if you don't stop that I'm gonna fall asleep," I mumble into his neck.

"Sleep, *Amica Mea.* I will keep you safe," he vows, as he runs his hand through my hair.

NINE

BELZAR

After what happened with *Chad* last night, I don't want to take any chances, so I ride with Maddy to work. If he shows up again I'll be here. I even have her bring an orange soda and miniature bottle of whipped cream vodka with her so she can summon me later if she needs to. I won't leave her safety to chance. Who knows what he'll do to her if I'm not around.

"What do you do if you see him?" I ask her for the hundredth time this morning.

"I tell him to leave me alone or my demon boyfriend will kill him?" She's getting sassier by the minute and I love it.

"*No.* You don't say anything. You *summon* your demon boyfriend and let him take care of it."

Her musical giggles fill the car and I can't hide my smile.

"Demon boyfriend. I like it. I should introduce you as just my boyfriend though. Probably best to leave off the demon part," she snickers as she turns into the parking lot.

"Introduce me? Who are you going to introduce me to, *Amica Mea?*"

"Oh. Ummm, I don't know. I guess no one," she mutters dejectedly.

"Hey now, none of that. You can introduce me to anyone you want. Now that I've figured out how to appear human," I say with a self-deprecating laugh that earns me a smile.

"I'll have to introduce you to Reed eventually, but I don't think I'm ready for that right now," she groans as she slowly shakes her head.

"Well, damn, Mads you don't have to tell anyone about me if you don't want to." It's only partially a tease, it does kind of hurt my feelings that she wants to keep me a secret, but whatever.

"Belzar." She side-eyes me as she pulls into a parking spot, turning to face me after she puts the car in park. "I don't want to keep you a secret, idiot. Reed is just a little too much sometimes. I know he's going to try to poach you from me." She rolls her eyes with an amused smile.

And now I feel like the idiot she just accused me of

being. Of course, it's not that she's ashamed of me or something. She just wants me all for herself. I can handle that.

"Well, whenever you're ready to tell anyone about me, feel free. I'm gonna go home and continue to tell everyone about you. Now come kiss your boyfriend and get your cute ass to work," I order teasingly.

She laughs but does as I say, leaning over the armrest and kissing me thoroughly. It's going to be hours before she can see me again and she needs to get her fix before she leaves. I feel the same, so I meet her nip for nip, tongue swirl for tongue swirl. We finally break apart panting and I wipe her lips with my thumb.

"Go. Before I change my mind and don't let you go to work today." I growl, my voice husky with lust.

"Yes, Sir," she sasses.

My eyes turn and my nostrils flare at the honorific. I need to get out of here before I take her in her car, in the school parking lot. Looking around to make sure no one can see me, I kiss her one last time then vanish, reappearing in my room.

"Where've you been?" A deep rumbly voice startles me from the dark corner.

"Motherfucker! What the hell are you doing in here, Oz?" I growl at the asshole that surprised me.

"Well, I came in to check on you some time ago. Imagine my surprise when I found you gone... *again.* No one is telling me anything. I want answers. Where do you keep disappearing to? What do you *do* while you're there?"

"Oh, gee, I wonder why no one has told you anything? Couldn't be because you're an asshole, psycho and no one *wants* you to know what the fuck is going on," I snark.

"Well, gee, Belzar, are you doing something that would upset me?" he snarks right back.

"Everything upsets you, so yeah, probably." I shrug, not even caring if he can see it. I feel his eyes narrow at me and bite my lips together to contain my smirk. I love riling him up.

"Then you better get the fuck over here and apologize for whatever you've done."

"And if I don't?" I challenge.

"Then I'll chain you up so you can't run off when that bitch summons you again," he snaps.

When he calls Maddy a 'bitch', I see red, completely losing control. Rushing him, I grab him by his throat and slam him into the wall. "Don't you *ever* talk about her like that," I snarl. "I don't give a fuck who you are. I won't let anyone speak a derogatory word against her. Do you understand me?" I slowly squeeze his throat tighter and tighter, restricting his airflow.

His eyes are solid black and I can tell, despite the fact I know I'm hurting him, he's pissed. More pissed than I've ever seen him, but I can't let that stand. He tries to push me away, but I grab one of his hands with my free hand, and the other with my tail, and slam them into the wall too.

"I love her. You will accept that or get the fuck out of my life," I declare without a moment's hesitancy. I may love this asshole, but I will pick Madelyne every day.

He must see the resolve in my eyes because he starts to deflate. As he gives up the fight, I loosen my hold on him. Once I release his throat enough that he can breathe, he sucks down air then nods once, and walks out of the room. I allow it because I'm done with him right now. I don't even want to look at his face. I might get pissed off all over again and really hurt him this time.

Sinking onto the bed, I put my head in my hands, and elbows on my knees. I already regret what I said to Oz. I don't *want* him to get the fuck out of my life. I love the fucker, I do, but he's a fucking prick for pulling that shit and he knows it. I could chase after him and apologize, but he wouldn't learn his lesson if I did, so I just sit here in the dark wishing life wasn't so damn complicated. If only I knew just how fucking complicated shit was about to get.

A knock at my door pulls me from my thoughts and my head snaps up. Without waiting for a response, Zeph just strolls on in. Sighing, I scoot over on the bed making room for him. I've got a feeling we're gonna be here a while, might as well let him get comfortable.

"Everything okay? Oz seemed pretty upset when he stormed out of here," Zeph starts hesitantly.

"He confronted me about where I've been, said the wrong thing about Maddy, and I slammed him against the wall. I told him to accept that I love her or get the fuck out of my life," I explain deadpan.

"Wow. Okay. So it is serious with this chick. What'd you say her name was?"

"It's as serious as it gets. I made a vow to spend the rest of eternity making sure she feels loved and cherished."

"You *what?* How could you make that kind of vow to a human? What are you going to do when she *dies,* Belzar? You can't make sure she feels loved and fucking cherished if she's in fucking *Heaven!*" he exclaims, his voice getting louder and screechier the longer he rants.

"Well, I'll just have to corrupt her enough that she ends up here." I smirk.

"Oh sure, just condemn her soul, no biggie." He rolls his eyes exaggeratedly.

"Trust me, she'd rather be here with me. She already thinks it's going to happen just from being with me the other day. She's made her peace with it, might as well make it a reality."

"Do you hear yourself? You're tying yourself to a woman you've known for a few fucking hours. You really think that's a good idea?"

"If you knew her, you'd do the same thing. Actually, she told me last night she met you. I guess she accidentally summoned you too when she was harassed by some dick, as she was leaving work at the elementary school yesterday."

"No fucking way! *That's* your girl? Shit, she's hot.

How you feel about sharing?" He waggles his brows and I kinda want to punch him in his face. "Kidding, kidding," he assures me with his hands raised in surrender.

"I told her about you. About my relationship with all of you."

"Really? What'd she have to say about that?"

"She said she's okay with it. Like I told her all of *you* are okay with me being with her. Because you love me and you want me to be happy," I stress the last part.

"Of course we do, and you know Oz will come around eventually. Maybe he'll chill out if he meets her and can understand why you feel this way about her," he suggests. "Hell, now that I know the fucking goddess that summoned me earlier is your girl, *I* completely understand. I was only in her presence for a short time, but I can definitely see getting addicted to her. Think she'll summon me again?" He gives me his patented puppy dog look and as usual, I can't say no to that face.

"I'm sure she will, Zeph. You'll see her again soon. Don't worry." I pat his leg.

"Thanks. Maybe we can hang out at her house, the three of us." His face lights up at the thought. "We can do whatever it is you guys do when you're there."

I can't hold the laugh in. "I doubt we could do *exactly* what we do when I'm there, but we could figure it out for sure. She seemed pretty interested in our relationship. Maybe we could show her how we work together." I smirk as his face flushes.

"You really think she would like that?" His brows are almost in his hairline; they're raised so high.

"I think you'll both get along great when you spend some time together. Maybe too good actually. Hmmm, on second thought, you stay here. I don't want you to take my place," I tease.

"Has she told you she loves you yet?" At my glare then subsequent eye-roll and nod, he continues. "Then I don't think anyone could take your place, Belz."

"I know you're right, but it's just so odd how I feel about her. It's like I've known her for mere minutes but also all my life, at the same time. It makes no damn sense, but I'm not gonna fight it."

"You know, I had this strange sense of deja vu when I met her. Like I'd met her before, or she was somehow important to me. I don't know. It's ridiculous, but I felt this strong pull towards her when I appeared. That's actually why she ran into me. I was so entranced and confused by the feeling, I froze. I didn't even see the man she was talking to."

"Yeah, it was probably a good thing I stayed invisible the first time she summoned me. Devil knows what would have happened." I shudder just thinking about the possibilities. "That reminds me. That fucker that was harassing her, he's a demon. He showed up at her house when I was there and tried to scare me off with the whole eyes-changing thing. Too bad for him that didn't work this time. He was not expecting to come up against a much scarier demon." I can't hold back the self-satisfied smirk. I didn't tell Maddy that part of our interaction.

"The fuck? Another demon? Is she a fucking demon magnet or something?"

"I don't know, but I'd like to find out. Maybe I can do some research on summonings at work today. Speaking of, I better go. I'll see you later Z." I kiss him, then head to work, hopeful I'll get some fucking answers.

TEN

MADELYNE

"**M**addy! Maddy! Maddyyyy!" my best friend calls from down the hall, dragging out the end of my name on the third time he screeches it.

Stopping in my tracks, because I know it'll be much worse if I ignore him, I turn around with a tired smile on my face. I love Reed, I do. I have to remind myself that sometimes. "Yes, Reedy Bear?" I mostly love the nickname because he hates it so much, even though I think he secretly loves it.

"Bish! What did I tell you about calling me that in public? People can hear you, ya know?" He glowers at me. "Now, where in the Hell have you *been*? I swear I've hardly seen you all fucking week, girl. You *know* how I get when I don't get enough Maddy time. I'm gonna start telling people it's your fault I'm being crazy, and you know they'll believe me." He crosses his arms and juts out a hip, tilting his head at me with his lips pursed.

It's a good thing it's so early and there are no kids here yet. Also, no other teachers in this hall. Reed is always getting in trouble for his mouth. He has no control over it, I swear. I don't know how they let him be around kids every day.

"Trust me, you wouldn't believe me if I told you. This week has been bizarre, to say the least. But I do have some gossip to share if you want to hear it." I waggle my brows enticingly.

"Excuuuse me. You know damn well I want any and every bit of gossip, no matter who or what it's about." He lays the sass on thick, wagging his finger in front of him and bobbing his head.

I roll my eyes and shake my head, trying to hide my smile. He's a fucking nut, but he's my nut. "I've got a boyfriend," I sing-song.

"Shut your mouth! No, the fuck you don't," he argues dramatically.

"Pretty sure…" I draw out with my brows scrunched together like I need to think about it.

"Well, *I'm* pretty sure you would have told me if you were seeing someone. So I don't believe you," he pouts.

"I'm telling you right now, Reed. I just met him on Monday. It's not like I've been keeping him a secret for months or something, damn."

"You've known him three *days* and you're already calling him your boyfriend?!" he screeches. "Have you *slept* with him?" he gasps in hushed tones, putting his hand to his chest.

"Don't pretend to be a prude. We both know you would approve if I slept with him the first day." I roll my eyes.

"Okay, fine. That's true." He purses his lips as he holds up his hand in surrender. "Soooo, when am I gonna meet him?"

I groan and laugh at the same time. I totally saw this coming. "He's coming over tonight. Why don't you stop by? We can have dinner," I offer as the bell rings, signaling that students are now allowed in the building.

"Ugh. Fiiiine, I'll come by after work. Time to go watch some crotch goblins," he groans.

Laughing, I wave him off as I head into my classroom. It's going to be a long day, and now an even longer night.

I love getting to spend all day with my kids; watching them grow and learn new things, but where do they get all of that energy? If I weren't already over the whole going out and partying thing, working with kids all day would definitely do it. As is, I'm really looking forward to just relaxing with Belz again tonight. It's quickly becoming my nightly ritual to summon him as soon as I get home, then spend the night together.

Of fucking course, *then* I remember I invited Reed over for dinner to meet Belz. Definitely won't be getting that nice relaxing night I was hoping for. It took me a while to clean up my classroom today because poor Jessie had an accident right before the bell rang. So I'm running late, rushing to my car, not paying attention to my surroundings. That's always when things go to shit. I don't know why I do this to myself. Just as I get to my car I hear him call my name in the most sinister voice I've ever heard.

My spine stiffens at the sound. This isn't good. I just know this interaction won't be like last time. Fuck! I need to summon Belz, *now*!

"Well, well, well. Look what we have here. And all alone, not a soul in sight to help you this time." His voice sounds different, but I know without turning around that it's Chad.

Fumbling in my purse I grab the bottles, quickly opening them one after the other. I take a gulp of the orange soda then pour the vodka in, closing the lid and shaking the bottle. Can't say I've ever mixed a drink like this before, but Christ I hope it works.

"Hey, bitch, I'm talking to you," he growls as he grabs my shoulder and forcefully spins me around.

I gulp as I get a look at him. He's in his demon form and not near as handsome as he is as a human. He must do a lot more to look human than Belz does. Belz looks the same, just without the horns, wings, and tail, but Chad? As a human, he looks like the quintessential boy next door. As a demon, he is… ugly as fuck. No resemblance at all. It's no wonder he sounded different, his teeth are huge, pointy monstrosities, and his top lip is pulled up so high I'd be surprised if it ever actually touched his bottom. Where his eyebrows should be is a defined ridge that goes across his forehead in a wave. Like a bumpy squiggly line on his head. His eyes aren't black like Belz's either, they're this foggy white. His skin is the color of burnt toast, black with patches of brown, and he has pointed ears with ridges like the one on his forehead.

He's going on about something, but I'm not exactly paying attention, you know, because of the whole staring in horror thing. I catch something about my mom and I snap my head up. He's got my attention now, but suddenly he jerks his head to the left.

"Back off. She's *mine!*" he growls.

"Doesn't look like she feels the same way. Maybe it's time to find a new obsession." I hear from beside me, but I can't see anyone. It sounds like Zephyr though… Did I accidentally summon him again?

"Pretty sure I told you last fucking *night* that she was mine and to leave her the fuck alone," Belz snarls, gaining Chad's attention as he whips around to shoot daggers at him. Belz takes a menacing step toward him and Chad whirls on me.

"We're not done. We'll *never* be done. I don't care how many demons you fuck. You *will* be mine." With that, he disappears in a puff of smoke and I fall back against the car door.

"You okay?" A voice says beside me. I'm almost certain it's Zephyr, but I still can't see anyone.

"No offense, but I'd be doing a lot better if I wasn't talking to the invisible man. Mind letting me see you now?"

"Oh, yeah. Sorry," I can hear the grimace in his tone, then suddenly, I can *see* it.

"Oh good, it *is* you." I laugh.

"*Amica Mea!*" Belz calls as he storms up to me, then scoops me up in his arms. "I'm going to find him and kill him. Don't you worry about him. I promise I'll keep you safe," he vows.

"I know you will, Belz. Thank you for coming and saving me. I don't know what he was going to do, but it couldn't have been good. Why did he come to me as a demon? And holy hell. He was ugly! He didn't look anything like you do as a demon. I don't know what you look like, Zephyr, but I sincerely hope it's not as bad as

Chad." I shudder at the thought of this gorgeous man turning into something hideous like that.

"I don't know if I should feel flattered or insulted," he grumbles.

"Definitely flattered. She's obviously interested in you, otherwise, she wouldn't care if you look like a hideous monster in your demon form," Belz spills my secrets.

"Hey! Don't tell him that!" I cry, smacking my pain in the ass boyfriend in the chest.

"Am I wrong?" I know my glare is answer enough, but I can't help it. "That's what I thought. Now, let's get you home and you can get to know Zeph. See if that interest goes any further." The bastard has the balls to wink at me.

"Shut up and get in the car." I push him away and open my door. It's not until everyone's in and I'm pulling out of the school that I remember... "Oh! I invited Reed over for dinner, so that'll be fun," I announce.

"Who's Reed?" Zephyr asks from the back seat.

"My gay best friend. And he's going to eat you up. Especially since he's coming over to meet my *boyfriend*." I tilt my head toward Belz. "He's not gonna be expecting two new guys. He'll for sure think you brought a friend for a double date," I warn them. It's only fair.

"I don't know, two guys are plenty for me. I might be interested in adding a woman to the mix, but not another guy," Zephyr muses from behind me.

I flick my eyes to the rearview mirror, looking at him in shock. Surely I didn't hear him right. I don't even know which part of that I'm more shocked by. That he has two boyfriends or that he wants a girlfriend... and was he implying *I* would be the girl for that?

"Don't think about it too hard, *Amica Mea*. Smoke's about to come out of your ears. Just ask. Zeph will tell you anything."

"Dude. Did you just call her?" Zephyr asks in wonder.

Belz turns in his seat and I catch his glare out of the corner of my eye as I drive.

"Yeah, I did. You got a problem with that?" he asks rather hostilely.

I'm kind of curious about that myself. I mean, Zephyr is his boyfriend and has been for I don't even know how long. Surely he would have something to say about Belz calling me that, but he just smiles.

"Not even a little. I know you love me. You don't have to call me your love for me to know that. We've never really done the whole nickname thing before, so why would it bother me? She obviously means a lot to you for you to use those words. And not just in her language. In *our* language. It means something to *you*. Why would I have a problem with that? Besides, I have eyes." He rolls said eyes and shakes his head. The captain obvious comment makes no sense to me, but apparently, Belz understands.

"Yes, well, we both know you're not the one I'm worried about," Belz grumbles in reply.

"You don't think your other friends will like me?" I

chew on my bottom lip as I grip the steering wheel tighter. I don't know why I'm so upset at that thought. For some reason, it just feels like an all-or-nothing sort of thing. Like I can't just have Belz, I've gotta have Zephyr, his brother, and Oz, the asshole too. And if *they* say no, I'm kicked to the curb.

"I'm sure they will once they get to know you. And don't worry about Oz, he's a dickbag, but his feelings about you do not affect us. I've told him as much. He can either pull his head out of his ass and welcome you to the fold or he can get out of my life. You're stuck with me, *Amica Mea*. Nothing will keep us apart." Belz reaches over and grabs my hand as he makes the vow and I feel a shock where he's touching, that intensifies and spreads up my arm.

"Wh-what was that?" I stammer.

"That was a demon's vow. It's not the first I've made to you, but we weren't touching the first time, so you didn't feel it settle into place."

"And what happens if a demon's vow is broken? What if something out of your control comes between us?" I start to freak out. I don't want something bad to happen to him.

"Oh, look, we're home." His poor attempt to deflect my question earns a soft chuckle from our back passenger, but a side-eyed glare from me.

"You're not getting out of answering, Belzar. It's an important question and I deserve to know. In fact, no one is allowed to make a demon vow to me until I know exactly what that means," I declare. That same electric feeling I had when Belz touched me, erupts all over my body; I don't know *how*, since I'm not touching anyone. What the fuck is going on with me?

ELEVEN

ZEPHYR

I completely understand why Belz never wants to come home now. Being in Maddy's presence is like a drug. The more time you spend with her, the more you *want* to. I honestly don't even care that I'm stuck here watching the man I love wrapped around another person. Am I jealous? Hell yes, I'm jealous! I want to be Belz. I want to hold Maddy like that, run my hands along her arms, watching as goosebumps break out everywhere I touch. I want to kiss every inch of her soft skin, reveling in each shudder that passes through her, as my lips skim over her body.

"So, Zephyr, how long have you and Belz been together?"

Her words shatter the fantasy and bring me back to

reality. "A very long time. We don't tend to keep track, honestly," I answer with a shrug.

"Does time mean nothing to you?"

"Not really. Hell is mostly the same thing over and over, day after day. Time tends to run together. Makes the torture that much more unbearable." I wink at her.

"Why would you say that with a wink?" Belz groans.

"What? Hell's known for its torture, right?" I ask, shrugging my shoulders.

"Yes, Hell is very well known for its torturing. I believe what Belz is talking about is the wink makes it seem like you mean a different kind of unbearable torture." Maddy smirks at me.

"Hey, if that's what you're into, Doll, I can make it happen." I wink again, loving the blush that takes over her face. Sadly, our lovely bantering is interrupted by the doorbell.

"Right. No talk about torture of any kind and no demon or Hell talk either. Be normal *human* men for the night. Got it?" She demands.

"Damn, you're sexy when you're bossy." I groan.

"She is, isn't she?" Belz agrees with heated eyes.

Maddy just sighs and shakes her head. "Just behave, please."

"Yes, ma'am," we reply at the same time.

She climbs off Belz's lap and I check out her ass as she walks to the door. If Belz sees, he doesn't say anything.

She turns a corner and I can't see her anymore, so I sit back and relax until I hear a high-pitched squeal.

"I should be concerned, shouldn't I?"

"Yeah... probably." He doesn't even sound sorry that I'm going to have to deal with Maddy's friend hitting on me.

"Can I tell him I'm your boyfriend?" I whine. If *anyone* is going to be hitting on me, I want it to be Maddy, not her friend. Then again, maybe Maddy will get jealous when she sees him flirting with me and decide she wants me for herself. "You know what, never mind. Let's just wait and see how tonight pans out."

"You're up to something aren't you?" He glowers at me.

"Who, me? Not at all. Don't you worry one bit. I'm sure her best friend will love you," I tease him with an evil grin.

He doesn't have time to interrogate me though because they enter the living room and Maddy starts the introductions.

"Reed, this is Belz, my boyfriend. Belz, Reed."

"Okay. Pre-k pause," he cries while putting a hand out in front of him when he says pre-k and the other out when he says pause. "*That* is your boyfriend?! Giiiirl. You've been holding out on me. Dayuuum!" That's when he notices me and does this really creepy slow turn as he stares at me. "My, my. And *who* do we have here? Maddy! Did you bring me a snack? You're so thoughtful."

"That's Zephyr. He's... Belz's friend," she stammers over my introduction.

"Oh, friend, huh? Do you like men, *Zephyr?*" he purrs.

"On occasion," I admit.

"Well, if today isn't just my lucky day!" He claps with a huge smile on his face. "Now, what's for dinner? I'm *starving.*"

Oh shit. Why do I get the feeling he's not talking about food? I shoot Belz a panicked look but the fucker smirks at me with his twinkling fucking eyes. I swear I'll get him back for this.

"Actually, I made chicken carbonara and garlic bread," Belz announces.

"You did?" Maddy asks, looking at him like he's lost his mind.

"Yes, sweetie, I did." He looks at her like she should shut up, but you know in a nice way, then mutters "Sic erit," under his breath.

Maddy must hear him because her eyes widen and she quickly nods. "Yes, that's right. I completely forgot about that."

"You *forgot* your boy toy made dinner? How could you forget that? You feeling alright, dear?" Reed teases as he shakes his purple hair out of his eyes.

"They've been a little busy since she got home. Sounded like she forgot a lot of things. I'm not surprised she forgot that dinner was cooking." I wink at him and instantly regret it. Never wink at a man that's interested in you when you're not interested in him. Bad things can happen. I hope he's not the obsessive type.

"Well. Who knew Maddy was such the hussy. Glad I got here after fun time was over. I love you and all, but I don't wanna see that. Now if these two were the ones having fun I would gladly walk in on that any day. Mmmhmm, just imagining it has me all tingly."

"Well, thank you. I'm sure it'd be a show to remember." I can't hide my smirk at the thought. "Excuse me, I'll go set the table." Standing up, I ignore Belz's glare as I make my way to the kitchen. I know he could have set the table, but I needed a little break, and some things can be done without magic. Plus, this leaves him alone with Maddy's best friend and I can't wait for the inquisition to start.

"Sooo, how'd you meet?" I hear Reed ask in a sickeningly sweet voice, followed by stuttering as Belz tries to come up with an answer.

I don't think there is a nice way to say 'he's a demon that I accidentally summoned one night and we decided we liked each other, so he pops in every night so we can fuck.'

"We met on a dating app," Maddy chimes in.

"Really? I thought you hated those stupid apps." I can hear the skepticism in his voice as I get the plates out of the cabinet.

"I do. I downloaded it as a joke. But when *this face* messages you, you give it a chance."

The room fills with laughter and I just shake my head

as I put the plates on her table. The problem with this table is it's small, and the chairs are set up so there are two side-by-side on each long section. Which means we'll be sitting next to each other not all across from one another, and I don't think I'm going to get lucky enough to sit next to anyone other than Reed. Once I have the food on the table I call for the others to join me. When Maddy comes in, I offer her a chair and try to sit beside her, but fucking Belz checks me with his shoulder and steals my seat. Leaving me no choice but to sit next to a now-beaming Reed. Like seriously, this dude's face is lit up like a fucking Christmas tree. It's fucking creepy.

"Don't worry, hot stuff! I got a seat for you," he says with this shoulder wiggle and cheeky grin.

I force a smile and slide into the seat next to him.

"It's okay, sweetie. I don't bite. Unless you ask me to." He waggles his brows with a look that seems to be begging me to ask him just that.

"Reed! Don't make Zeph uncomfortable!" Maddy scolds him and I buzz at the nickname.

"Oh, you're no fun! He can handle a little flirting, can't you, sexy?" he asks, as he runs his hand down my arm.

I'm really loving the lasers that Maddy is currently shooting at Reed. Makes me think my plan is working, so I decide to see how far I can push her.

"Absolutely. I love flirting." I wink at him, then turn my attention to the pasta in front of me.

"A man after my own heart!" he sighs dramatically with his hand to his chest.

"Okay, can we just eat now?" Maddy rolls her eyes and shakes her head, then grabs the tongs, placing some pasta on her plate.

"You okay, *Amica Mea?*" Belz leans in and whispers into her ear.

She shoulders him away and stabs at her noodles, taking a pretty aggressive bite of her carbonara and pointedly ignoring his question.

We all quietly serve ourselves and begin eating as the tension ratchets up more and more with every bite. Deciding to break the unbearable silence I turn to Reed.

"So, Reed, how'd *you* meet Maddy?"

The woman in question snaps her head up and points at him. "Don't you dare," she growls.

Reed just chuckles in response. "It was Maddy's first day at school, as a teacher. She had just graduated and-"

"Reed. Don't do it. I have plenty of stories about you too you know," she warns.

Of course, he doesn't heed her warning. "So it's the first day of school and we teach the loveliest little bunch of demons…"

I swear my eyes almost bug out of my sockets. I turn to Maddy and Belz with a look that clearly shouts 'Oh my god what the fuck! He knows about demons?!' Maddy quickly shakes her head and I can breathe again.

"Anyway, this one angel was not having a good day. Like everything that could go wrong for her, *did*. She spilled paint water all over Maddy's shoes. She had an accident and got shit *everywhere*. Then after lunch, she threw up all over Maddy. I mean she covered her! Luckily, I had a spare change of clothes in my room next door, because Maddy here was not prepared. Of course, she had to go the rest of the day looking like a hungover gay man, but at least she was puke-free."

"You know, you could have just said we met at work. You *really* didn't have to tell them how awful my first day was." She glowers.

"I could have, but where would the fun be in that?" he responds with a laugh.

Poor Maddy is bright red and blotchy. I can tell she's not happy he told us that story, but she must know it doesn't make us look at her any differently, so I don't know why she's that embarrassed about it. Still, I can't have my angel be upset, so I decide to tell her a story of my own.

"Don't feel so bad, Maddy. Sometimes we have prank wars at the house and this one time, Oz thought it would be funny to collect the dog's shit and hide it in my bed. I should have been more suspicious that he volunteered to walk him for a week, but I was just glad it didn't fall on me like usual."

Belz is sputtering across from me and I glare at him. He thought it was the funniest thing to ever come from our prank wars. Maybe it's time I turn the table and cover his room in hound shit.

"Oh, no! That's awful, Zeph! Did you get him back?" she asks and she sounds so ferocious, angry on my behalf, it's the sexiest I've ever seen her.

"Oh, I got him back alright. That's a story for another day though." I smirk at her.

"I'll hold you to it," she tells me with a wicked grin.

Oh, you can hold me alright... I mean, fuck, that's not even what she said, but she mentioned me and holding in the same sentence and that's just where my mind went.

Everyone finishes eating and Belz and I jump up to clean the mess.

"Well, as fun as this has been, I gotta go. Told Mikey I'd meet him for drinks," Reed sighs, dramatically rolling his head in a circle. "But you..." he says pointing at Maddy, "have some more tea to spill tomorrow. Don't think I'll let you get off easy either. That's his job." he smirks and tilts his head to Belz. "And maybe *his* too." He looks me up and down with a knowing grin.

"Shut up and get out of here," Maddy laughs, pushing him toward the door. "Tell Mikey I said hiii," she sing-songs.

"Oh yeah, I'm totally going to ruin the evening by bringing *you* up. He may not be as hot as your guys, but I'd still like to get some tonight, and I apparently have to lower my standards to do that," he huffs.

"It was lovely to meet you, Reed. If it matters at all, I

don't think you need to lower your standards. I think you're a funny, attractive man, and any guy would be lucky to have you. For a night or a lifetime. Don't sell yourself short," I squeeze his shoulder as he passes me.

"Wellll, if *that's* the case... why don't you come home with me and leave these two love birds alone." He wiggles his brows at me.

"Reed! Get!" Maddy scolds and we both burst out laughing.

"I guess that answers that question." He smirks at me. "Good luck with that," he stage-whispers, then rushes out the door laughing like a hyena as Maddy chases after him with a shoe.

Well, okay then. Guess tonight was a success.

TWELVE

MADELYNE

I swear I'm going to kill him, but at least he seemed to approve of Belz... and Zephyr, even if he did spend the whole dinner flirting with him and would gladly take him home. I don't know why that thought bothers me so much, but here we are. Belz didn't seem upset earlier when he said I was interested in his *friend*. He even implied he would be okay with me doing something about that interest. I'm not sure about how their relationship works. Could I really be in a relationship like that? Be with more than one man... demon, at a time?

"What are you thinking so hard about over here?" Belz asks, wrapping his arms around me from behind.

I can't help but sigh and melt into his big strong arms. I have never felt safer than when I'm in his arms.

"Just thinking about what you said earlier... About Zephyr..." I trail off, not knowing how to voice my thoughts.

"Ahhh. About your feelings for him, *Amica Mea?*"

I just turn my head and nod, not trusting my voice, or wanting him to see the uncertainty in my eyes. Of course, he doesn't let me hide from him. Moving his hands to my hips and spinning me to face him, he grabs my chin and lifts my head til our eyes meet, not letting me look away.

"I'm used to sharing *Amica Mea.* I know you are not, but it's all I know. I would love nothing more than to have you to myself for all of eternity, but to share you with the only men I trust? That could only intensify our relationship. It will bring us closer together, not push us apart. If you have no interest in any of them, that's fine, but don't ever feel like you need to hide your feelings. You want to kiss Zeph? Just to see what it would be like? Do it. You don't need my permission, but I'll gladly give it. Only when it comes to Zephyr, Zarreth, and Oz, though. Don't think I'm going to be okay with you and Chad getting together or something," he arches a brow and I just shake my head and roll my eyes.

"Did I hear something about kissing Zeph?" The man in question scares the shit out of me by sneaking up behind me.

"God damn it, Zeph! Don't *do* that!" I whirl around and smack him. "You gave me a fucking heart attack!"

"Sorry, Angel. Was not my intention."

Ugh. I can't stay mad at that damn puppy face. That's not fair. How am I ever going to be able to tell him no?

"Does he do this a lot? This face? It's not very demon-like," I tell Belz.

"All the time. He's too damn sweet to be a demon. Especially considering his line of work."

"Oh? What does he do? What do you do?" I turn and ask the demon himself.

"I'm part of the royal security. I'm actually one of the heads, my brother being the other. We have a link to the royal line. I do various special things to keep them safe," he answers rather vaguely.

"Interesting. What about you, Belz? What do you do in Hell?" I ask with a smile, excited to learn more about my boyfriend.

"I'm the head of communications with the royal security. Guess Zeph forgot he and Zarreth weren't the only ones in a leadership role." He glares at the demon in question.

"Oh, shut up. I just didn't know if you were going to tell her. I kept it very vague, okay?" Zeph retorts with an eye-roll.

"So you all work in security? Seems like an important job. Is that why you're on a first-name basis with the devil?" I ask Belz.

"You talked to her about Luc?"

"We were watching *Little Nicky*. Of course, I talked about him. You can't watch that movie and not think about him, or the blowout with Droxley and Bartleby," he argues.

Zeph laughs at that. "True. And yes, to answer your question, that's why we're on a first-name basis with Lucifer," he tells me.

"When are you going to tell me more about Hell? I want to know everything about where you're from."

"We'll talk about it soon, okay, *Amica Mea*?" He looks at me with pleading eyes and just like Zeph and his puppy dog eyes, I can't say no to him.

"Fine, but you should definitely make it up to me tonight," I tease him, licking my lips as I look up at him.

His eyes go black and I squeal as he throws me over his shoulder and starts walking down the hall to my room.

"Right, well I'm just gonna go home," Zephyr mumbles.

I smack Belz's ass and he stops walking. Pushing myself up so I can see, I give Zeph my best flirty look. "Or you could join us… if you want," I bite my lip as I wait for his reaction to my offer.

He slowly struts over, stopping right in front of me. "If you're sure you want me, there's nowhere else I'd rather be."

I gulp at the conviction in his voice, but quickly nod before he thinks it's a bad gulp. I've just never had anyone, besides Belz of course, tell me so adamantly that they want me. It's a little overwhelming but in a good way. His eyes turn black like Belz's do and he cups my face as I hold myself up, running his thumb over my lips.

"Anything you want, Angel." His voice goes all husky and my lady bits flutter at the promise.

Smacking Belz's ass I shout, "Onward good steed!"

He smacks my ass back, but then we're bouncing down the hallway, so I don't care. It's not long before he's flinging me over his shoulder and tossing me on my bed. I bounce several times before I settle, wiggling in anticipation as I watch the demons stalking me.

"If at any time, you change your mind and want either of us to stop, you just say so, *Amica Mea*," Belz orders.

"I will, but I won't. Now strip. I haven't seen you naked in *hours*."

Their dark laughter fills the air and I shiver in giddy excitement as I watch both of them remove their clothing in perfect synchronicity. Their toned bodies are so different, but both incredibly sexy in their own way. Belz is bigger than Zephyr, and thus thicker all over, from his broad chest to his thick thighs. Zeph is leaner, but every muscle is as equally defined as Belz's. While I'm drooling, counting the ridges of each plane on their bodies, they drop their pants, their hard cocks springing forth, pulling my attention from the deep V I was just admiring.

Remember how I said Belz was thick everywhere? Yeah, he's thick *there* too. As expected, Zeph is thinner but *damn*. What he lacks in girth, he more than makes up for in length. He even has a fancy peen, too! His ridges are different from Belz's, but they look like they would be enjoyable. The only way I can describe this dick is bejeweled. Instead of Belz's ridges, Z has smaller circles all over that look like the dildo of my dreams.

I lick my lips, imagining having that in my mouth, in my pussy, my ass. Mmmm so many ways for me to play with that. While I'm distracted by the sight before me, they share a look then turn to me, crawling up the bed, Belz kissing up my right leg while Zeph does the same to the left, pushing my skirt up as they go. Once they reach the top of my thighs, they each grab a side of my waistband, pulling my skirt and panties down my ankles. I've gotta say, I'm a fan of this whole working together thing.

They stop for a minute, just staring down at my naked pussy, then as one, they run a hand up each of my legs, spreading them wide. Which is good because soon I have two heads between those spread legs. I squeal as I feel two tongues swipe up my opening and twirl around my clit. I can't tell if they're kissing each other and my pussy just happens to be between them, or if they're battling over who gets to slurp up my juices. Either way, I am here for it.

All rational thought flees my head when a thick finger pushes into me, followed immediately by a thinner one. Both tongues continue to drive me crazy as their fingers stroke my pussy walls in tandem. Their other hands are squeezing my thighs as they pin them out of their way. As if their tongues and fingers weren't enough, the firmness with which they hold me open for them is enough to have me on the verge of release.

"Oh, God. Fuck. Jesus fucking Christ! What are you doing to me?" Fuck, I don't care what they're doing, as long as they never stop.

And they don't. The smart men... demons, that they are, take that for a rhetorical question and somehow double down on their ministrations. I swear I'm seconds away from going blind from too much pleasure. That's a thing right? Fuck, I'm sure it is. The way they work together to bring me to the edge over and over, before finally letting me fall off the cliff that is my orgasm, is a thing of beauty. I think they've convinced me of the joys of having more than one demon.

They finally sit up with smug as fuck looks on their faces as I lie there panting, after nearly meeting God by way of demons.

"Delicious. I could eat you for every meal, every day," Zeph groans.

I cover my face and silently whine into my hands until they're ripped away and I reluctantly open my eyes only to come face to face with Belz's black stare.

"Why are you embarrassed by that, *Amica Mea*? It's a compliment, no?" he asks with furrowed brows.

Sighing, I shake my head. "Yes, Belz, I suppose that could be considered a compliment. I'm just not used to men talking like that, okay?"

"Well then, we'll just have to get you used to it, won't we?" he retorts with a smirk on his too handsome face.

"You like dirty talk, Angel? You want me to use my tongue in every way to make you blush? I can handle that," Zeph asserts with a smile.

I just roll my eyes. "You know what I really want?" I purr.

"What's that?" he asks earnestly as he kneels on the bed.

"I want... you... to fuck me." I couldn't be any more blunt, but sometimes that's what it takes to get through to guys.

I was right of course, because his eyes, which were back to normal if a little heated, instantly turn black and he surges forward, blanketing my body and knocking Belz out of the way. He covers my mouth with his, stealing my breath with his kiss. Our groins line up and he grinds his cock on my dripping pussy, occasionally slipping through my folds because I'm so wet. When his head bumps my clit I shudder, wrapping my legs around his waist.

I have to imagine he wants me as badly as I want him because he doesn't take his time, or try to tease me. He pulls his hips back and thrusts forward, just sliding right in. I suppose that's a perk of not being so thick.

"Oh, yes. Fuck me, Zeph!" I beg as I squeeze my legs around him.

"Devil, you feel so damned good," he groans, as he plunges into me over and over. "Fuck, Angel. You're gripping me so tight, your pussy is pulsing around my cock. Fuck! Tell me you're there, and if you're not, you need to get there," he growls, before reaching down and rubbing my clit, setting me off.

"Yes! Yes! Oh, holy shit, yesss!" I scream as I explode all over him, feeling his hot cum shoot deep inside me.

I'm so glad I asked him to stay. Fuck, that was good. I'm laying here, all blissed out from the out of this fucking world orgasm my second demon just gave me, yes, I'm officially claiming Zephyr, when Belz's roar pulls me from my happy place.

"What in the fuck is *that?!*"

I open my eyes to see a livid Belzar pointing at Zephyr's back. "What? What's wrong?!" I start to panic. Did I fuck something up by fucking him? Oh my god! What did I *do?!*

"This fucker has a *mate* mark! How the hell did you get that?! *When* did you get it? Who's your fucking mate, you fucking bastard?" The more he talks the more enraged he becomes.

I look up at Zeph, who's still hovering over me, and find him staring at me in wonder. "Zeph?" I entreat.

"It's you, Angel. *You're* my mate," he whispers in awe.

"But how? Wh-what does that even *mean?*" I start asking the million questions running through my mind, but I'm silenced by a soft kiss on, my forehead.

"Shhh, I'll explain everything, my love, but I need to check on Belz."

Belz. Fuck. I snap my head to the side looking for him. He's angrily pacing the room, muttering something I can't quite make out and throwing his hands in the air. Zeph jumps up and walks over to him, his head tilting as he gets closer like he's looking at something. I don't know what the fuck is going on, to be honest with you. When he reaches Belz and puts his hand on his shoulder, Belz freaks out, whirling around and punching Zeph in the face.

"Oh my God! Belzar! What the fuck?" I screech.

"No! You were *mine!* You *are* mine. He can't just fucking take you from me. I'll fucking die, *Amica Mea.* Don't you see? I can't fucking live without you. But you're *his* fucking mate! He's not going to want to share you with me now."

"Don't I have a fucking say? This is my fucking life. I get a fucking say in who I spend it with. If *I* want you, it doesn't matter what Zeph wants."

"That's not how it works, *Amica Mea.* Not in demon society. By demon law, if your mate says I can't see you anymore then that's it." He shrugs helplessly.

I turn to Zeph and glare at him. "You wouldn't do that, would you? You wouldn't take my choice away from me like that." I feel like I'm burning alive just at the thought of not seeing Belz anymore. He says he would die without me, but I think *I* would die without *him.*

"Of course not, Angel. Besides-"

"See. I told you he wouldn't be that stupid. It's fine. Calm down."

"It's not *fine,* Madelyne. Don't you see?"

"Will someone fucking listen to me?" Zeph cuts in before Belz can get heated again.

"What, Zeph?"

"I was saying… it doesn't matter because you're *his* mate too."

Wait, what?

Belz must be as surprised by that as I am because he whirls on him. "What are you fucking talking about? I saw the marks. She's *your* mate."

"Yes, she is. But she's yours too, you idiot. Look. You have markings here too. You've probably had them since the first time you two slept together, but you couldn't see it," he explains.

Belz freezes. I don't think he's even breathing. "You're… you're sure?" The words are so soft I can barely hear them.

"I'm sure. Maddy, you have a camera?"

"Yes!" I exclaim, jumping up and running out of the bedroom to get my phone. I return shortly after, already turning the camera on as I walk over to them. I finally get a look at Belz's back and gasp at what I see.

There's a series of intricate lines that look to form some kind of flame with a swirling center. It's really fucking cool.

I quickly take a picture then turn to do the same to Zephyr, running my fingers over his mark before taking the photo. He has the same mark, but the tip of the flame is pointing to the right, while Belz's is pointing up. Once I show Belz the pictures he collapses on the bed. He sits there, staring at nothing for a while before he speaks again.

"So, we're *both* her mates?" he asks hopefully.

I know I haven't known him long, but I couldn't even imagine losing him.

"That's what I was *trying* to tell you!" Zeph cries.

Hesitantly, I walk over to Belz. When I get close enough, he snaps a hand out and pulls me into him, banding his arms around me and burying his face in my chest.

"I thought I was going to lose you," he mumbles.

"You'll never lose me, Belz," I assure him, as I run my fingers through his long hair.

"But what are the fucking odds we'd both be her mates?" I hear Zeph mutter to himself.

"Let's go to bed, okay? It's been a long day and I just want to lie between my two *mates.*" I test out the word. It's a little weird, but I think I like it. I can definitely get used to being between these two.

We crawl into bed, me laying my head on Belz's chest and Zeph wrapping himself around my back. I feel so at home in their arms, like nothing can touch me as long as they're here. It's so peaceful, I fall asleep almost instantly. The last thing I hear before I drift off into dreamland is Zeph vowing to scour Hell to find out who Chad is and why he wants me so badly.

THIRTEEN

ZEPHYR

I stayed up all night. I couldn't make myself fall asleep, no matter how comfortable I was, my brain would not shut off. Do you know how fucking rare demon mates are? I don't think I actually know any. Hell, we wouldn't know anything about mates or marks if it weren't for Belz's job. To think Maddy is not just my mate, but Belz's too? Honestly, I think only Hell royalty has ever had more than one mate.

The more I thought about it as I laid there with my beautiful one-of-a-kind mate in my arms, the more convinced I became that something was going on here. Add in the fact a low-level demon is trying to claim her... There has to be something special about her that we don't know. *Yet.* I'm damn sure going to figure it out though.

We see Maddy off to work then head home. We decided this morning we weren't going to tell anyone about Maddy or the mate marks. I'm going demon hunting and Belz is going to see what else he can learn about mates from his boss.

"Good luck today. Be careful with your questions. I don't want anyone to catch on to what she is to us," I tell him for the millionth time.

"Yes, Dad. I know. You're the one that needs to be careful. Going to the outskirts? That's fucking dangerous, Zeph."

"You think I don't know that? What the fuck else am I supposed to do? We have to find this fucker. That's where his kind stays, so that's where I'll go. I'll go anywhere and do anything for Maddy. I don't care how stupid or dangerous it is. She deserves answers, Belz. Even to the questions she doesn't know to ask."

He stops arguing with me after that. He would gladly go with me, but he's the only one that can talk to his boss, she keeps to herself so much she won't talk to anyone else, and we need all the information we can get from her.

"If I'm not back by tomorrow... then you can come looking for me, but I'll be fine. We'll figure this out together, Belz." I give him a fierce hug before leaving. Unlike him, I don't have wings, so it'll take me some time to get there and I have no time to waste.

"Wait! Take Fireball with you." He stops me before

I've taken three steps, not even waiting for a response, before he whistles for the Hellhound.

Fireball comes bounding down the steps, running so fast I have my doubts he'll be able to stop. Doubts that are validated when he crashes into me and sends me flying backward. Fucker may be a puppy, but he's *huge*. Hellhounds are nothing like Earth dogs. For one, his nose comes up to my navel when he stands. His fur is shaggy and pitch black, I mean so dark you won't be able to see him if he steps in a shadow. His eyes burn blue with Hellfire and he can light his entire body on fire with a thought. He may be the sweetest hound I've ever known, but he's also the most loyal, protective, and deadly. There's a reason Belz wants me to bring him with me, he's killed his fair share of asshole demons.

"Alright, alright, get off me you big mutt," I grumble, as I push the oversized pup off my chest, then stand up. The fucker just looks at me, head tilted and this knowing fucking look on his face. "Yes, okay? We're going on a fucking hunt."

He starts howling merrily, running circles around me, as I simply stand there shaking my head.

"Yeah, yeah. Let's go already. Tell Belz bye."

In response he runs up to Belz, putting his front two paws on his chest, and proceeds to lick his entire face, covering it with hound saliva. I can't stop my laugh as he tries to get the hound off of him. Finally, Fireball has had enough and is ready to get on with his journey because he backs up and runs back to me. Getting a mouthful of my shirt, he pulls me in the direction we need to go. Did I mention he was a smart fucker?

We leave Belz behind as we head west. Once Fireball knows I'm coming, he lets go and runs ahead. We make our way to the city gates where the guard gives us a bewildered look and stops us when we get closer.

"Hey, Zephyr, where are you going?" he asks.

"The outskirts," I reply briskly.

"The fuck you going there for?" His brow ridge furrows as he looks at me like I'm a special kind of stupid.

"Got some business I need to take care of with a lowlife. Where the fuck else would I go to find him?" I snark.

"Yeah, that'd be the place. Hope you kill some of those fuckers while you're there. Try not to get dead yourself, Zephyr."

"Count on it, old man," I reply with a smirk. Sonnoz is a good guy, never complains about getting the shitty jobs like guarding this gate that no one ever uses. It's no wonder he gave me a weird look.

He just shakes his head as he opens the door for Fireball and me. "You take care of him, Fireball. Don't let him get lost," he orders my hound.

Fireball huffs at him, blowing smoke out of his nose. Oh, no. He feels slighted. We need to get out of here before he decides to take a bite out of Sonnoz. I grab him by the scruff and drag him through the gate.

"Thanks, Sonnoz. See ya later," I holler as I get Fireball as far from the demon as possible. I can't say it was very smart for him to question my hound's ability to protect his master. Even if that's not what he was meaning at all.

As soon as we step out of the city's barrier, the hellscape changes. Inside of the gates looks about as close to an Earth city as you can get. This side of the gate though? This is the barren wasteland one would expect to see in Hell. There aren't different levels of Hell as many Earth books would have you believe, but there are lots of distinct areas. Each one is more dangerous than the next.

As we're walking across the hot, red, Hell desert, I see the landscape shimmering in the distance.

"We're almost to the Waremis Ice Fields, boy," I warn Fireball. He just growls and wags his tail in response. "Yeah, what do *you* have to worry about? It's not like you can freeze or anything," I grumble. No, I can't fucking freeze either, but it gets really fucking cold, okay? It's not like a trip to the spa.

We trudge through the snow and ice, correction, *I* trudge through the snow and ice. Fireball is running around, jumping into snow piles, and howling like he's having the time of his life. He's way too happy right now. Or maybe I'm just grumpy because it's fucking *cold.* Some time later I finally see the shimmer that signifies the next hellscape.

The next leg of our trip will lead us through the

Moaning Forest, aptly named for all the lost souls wailing their afterlife away. We weave our way through trees with low-hanging scraggly branches that like to try to grab anyone that gets too close. The burn from these trees' touch is not fun, so we take extra care to avoid them. We're making good progress when one of those stupid fucking spirits flies up to Fireball's face and starts taunting him. I reach out to grab him before he can take off after it, but I was so focused on him and the spirit, I forgot to pay attention to the damn trees.

Just as I'm extending my arm to grasp the hound, a thin limb wraps around it, causing me to cry out in pain. Hearing my scream, Fireball turns his attention to me and charges the tree, blue hellfire exploding from his fur. He easily gets his giant jaws around the branch that has ahold of me, biting it in two. No longer attached to the tree of death, the branch crumbles off my arm, falling to a pile of ash at my feet.

Fireball turns off the hellfire as he cautiously approaches me. As soon as he gets close enough, he sniffs and then licks my wound, drawing another howl from me.

"Jesus, *fuck*, Balls! That fucking *hurts*. Warn a demon, would ya?" I gripe as he continues to lick my wound. It's finally starting to feel better. Thank fuck for hellhound's healing saliva.

Once he's satisfied he's done all he can do, he steps back, admiring his handiwork. He definitely deserves the smug as fuck look on his little hound face. Before he started licking it, it was already festering, with nasty boils popping up all around my forearm. Now, I may have a scar, but it doesn't hurt so much anymore and I will be keeping my arm. So that's good.

"Thanks, Balls." I bend over and wrap my arms around him. He loves affection; pets and cuddles, and he deserves a fucking hug after that.

We're able to make it out of that fucking forest without further issues. Word spread through the spirits and trees what Fireball did to the tree that attacked me. Guess it was enough to convince the rest to leave us the fuck alone. As soon as we're clear of the forest, the next hellscape shimmers up ahead.

Walking through the Hell magic separating the hellscapes, we finally come up on a small camp of demons. Fireball walks closer to me in a protective stance. If anyone tries to attack, they'll be sorry. Not that I think any of these demons would be stupid enough. It's obvious looking at me, that I'm an upper-level demon and could burn their homes to the ground with a flick of my hand. Many of them duck into their huts as we walk closer, one who looks like he might be some kind of leader or something, stands tall before me. Well, as tall as he can at least, he's still shorter than me and has to look up at me. Stopping in front of him, I decide to get straight to the point.

"I'm looking for someone. He stole something from me, and I intend to get it back," I growl with a murderous look on my face. "Tell me his name and where I can find him and I won't burn your village to the ground." At the demon's curt nod, I go on, describing what the fucker looks like. His eyes flash with recognition. "You know him."

"Yes, but he hasn't been here in some time. Last time he was here, he said he found his golden ticket to get out of this place and get the acceptance he thinks is owed to him. I don't know where you can find him. Probably Earth," he shrugs.

"Golden ticket? What's that mean?"

"I don't know. He said he was on Earth and caught this woman's scent. Said she didn't smell human. That's all he would tell me. He didn't want anyone to know too much about her. Just said she was special and he was going to make her his." He shakes his head.

"Give me a name," I demand.

"Ugch'radd."

I nod once, thank him for his help, then turn and leave. *He has to be talking about Maddy. He could smell her? She's not human? What the fuck is going on?* I have to get back to Belz, tell him what I learned, and see if he has any new information to share.

FOURTEEN

BELZAR

I'm worried about Zeph, but I know he'll be fine now that Fireball is with him. If he manages to get hurt, Fireball can heal him, so that helps my anxiety about sending him to the outskirts alone. Yes, I know he can handle himself, it's part of his job after all, but it's natural to worry about the people you love when they're in dangerous situations. Now, it's time for me to see what Zofina can tell me about mates.

Flying across the city, I look down on the denizens of Gehenna. One thing about living here that has always brought me comfort, things rarely change. Demons mill around the square, trading goods, while others rush to do their Hell duties.

Landing in front of the castle, I march up to the doors

like I own the place. I know my place on the totem pole, so I'm under no illusion that's the truth, but arrogance and alpha posturing is the only way to survive here. Especially in the castle. I can't let any of these fuckers think for a second that I don't belong, that I just work here like they do. I *am* special, and they'll never forget that. The guard is quick to open the door before he loses his hand for not doing his job, and I stroll inside.

I stride down the familiar hallway to the purple door, knocking twice before opening it. I'm not surprised to see the princess alone. She despises everyone in this Godforsaken city except me for some reason.

"Belzar! You're coming in later and later every day. That doesn't have anything to do with a certain someone you won't tell me about, summoning you does it?" she teases me with a smirk as I walk into her room.

"Your Majesty," I bow my head in deference even though I know she hates it.

"You little shit," she growls then throws something at me.

I know it's coming, so I lean out of the way and her glass shatters against the wall behind me. "Now, that's no way to welcome an old friend," I tease.

"Maybe not, but it *is* the way to welcome an asshole like you," she responds with a smirk. "Now when are you going to tell me who keeps summoning you?"

"Straight to the point as always, Zofina. It's one of the things I love about you."

"Careful, Belz. Don't want Father to hear that, he'll start to get ideas," she groans.

Her father has been trying to get her to date one of us for eons. It's their one point of contention... well, besides that other thing that we don't talk about.

"Oh, please! He knows that's never going to happen, besides I have a mate now, so it's completely off the table. That's actually why I'm here. I need to know everything, Zo."

Her eyes widen and she jumps out of her seat. "What do you mean you have a mate? How? Who?"

"If I tell you, you must promise not to tell anyone, and tell me everything I need to know about them and the bond," I demand.

"Yes, yes. Of course, now tell me!" She waves me off, eager to hear my story.

"As you've no doubt suspected, I was summoned by a woman. I've been summoned by the same woman four times now, the first two were accidents. The first time she summoned me, I remained hidden and watched her all night. I became captivated by her."

"Belzar! You creeped on some poor girl? Shame on you!"

"If you don't stop interrupting me, I won't tell you the rest of it," I threaten with my brow raised in challenge.

"Ugh, you're such a spoilsport," she grumbles as she sits back in her plush wingback chair.

"The point of this conversation, why I need to know more about mates, is I'm not her only one."

Her jaw drops and her eyes are so wide it would be comical if this weren't so serious.

"Who? How many? Where is she? What's her name? Belzar, *tell me*. Please." She pelts me with questions and begs me to answer without allowing me to do so.

"Zo! Calm down. What's going on? Why are you freaking out right now?"

She attempts to compose herself, taking deep breaths and holding them, before releasing them. "Do you know what having multiple mates means?" she asks when she's finally collected enough to do so.

"I have my suspicions, but that's why I came to *you*."

"A demon having multiple mates is extremely rare. In fact, Father is the only one that's ever had more than one mate. For this woman to have two, she can't be a normal human woman. She's a demon, Belzar."

I'm not surprised to hear my thoughts confirmed. It's not unheard of for a demon to have a human mate, but for two demons to have the same mate is, especially if that mate is human. I knew last night, there was no way Maddy was human.

"But why would a demon be on earth? And she knew nothing about demons. Granted she wasn't terrified of me the first time she saw me in my demon form, but trust me, she knows *nothing* about demons or Hell."

"I believe she's a half-demon that was raised on earth

by her human parent… If I'm right, her human *father*," she emphasizes.

"Why would you think that?"

"Several years ago, I escaped Gehenna. I found my mate on Earth and lived blissfully for some time. Not near long enough, but my love gave me the most precious gift, a baby. We were a happy little family, until one day, my sweet Madelyne found my necklace. She didn't know its importance, she just thought it was a pretty trinket that she wanted to put in her mouth. The chain held a pendant that concealed my location from Gehenna. No one knew where I was or how to find me. But the moment that chain snapped, a beacon was sent here, telling the guards of my location.

"I had to leave. I couldn't let Father send his men after me. They would have killed Robert and our sweet baby. I couldn't let that happen. I had to protect them. So I left. Robert never knew what I was, I couldn't tell him. I couldn't tell him I was leaving so the devil wouldn't kill him and torture him for eternity. It was safer for them if I just returned to Gehenna. So that's what I did.

"Father was thrilled I had returned, but he was also angry. So angry. As part of my punishment for leaving, he made sure I could never do it again. I've been stuck here, not able to see the man I love. I haven't seen my daughter since that day. I stopped keeping track of time so I wouldn't know how big she had gotten without me. It hurt too much to even *think* about her. But here you are. Telling me my sweet baby girl has grown into a woman and is your mate. What are the odds, Belzar? That my daughter and my best friend would be mates?"

My heart stops beating, my mouth is so dry I couldn't talk if I wanted to. I stand there, stupefied as she tells her story, putting the pieces together as she talks. Maddy, my beautiful, awkward mate. She's the fucking granddaughter of Hell.

FIFTEEN

MADELYNE

I tried to summon Belz when I got home like I have every day this week, but he didn't show. I don't know if I'm suddenly doing something wrong or what, but I swear I'm mixing the drink exactly the same way. But no matter how many times I try, there's no cloud of smoke signaling his arrival. Now I have a coffee table full of Dreamsicles and nothing to do with them. I don't have a death wish, so sadly I won't be drinking them.

I'm really starting to get worried about him. I know he wanted to find out more about the whole mate thing, but he said he'd be here when I summoned him. I was under the impression that he couldn't resist the summons regardless of where he was or what he was doing. That's the only reason I wasn't freaking out all day about them being back in Hell. I don't even know *how* to summon Zeph.

Pacing around my apartment, I stop when a box on the shelf catches my eye. Figuring it's as good a distraction as any, I pull the box down and sit on my couch to examine it. It's been a long time since I looked at this box. I never told Dad I took it, but I'm sure he knows. He would definitely notice any of his preciouses missing. Dad loved Mom so fucking much he couldn't let go. Even after she just up and left us when I was a baby, he couldn't move on. His life would have been over when she left had it not been for me.

He was so heartbroken when he found her gone, but then I cried in my crib and he knew he didn't have the luxury to break down. He may not have my mom for whatever reason, but he had *me* and I was a piece of her. At least that's what he always told me. He made it no secret who my mother was. He didn't try to erase her from his life, in fact, he probably went a little too far to the other side. He made a shrine to her. He told me everything about her. For the longest time, I felt close to this woman I had never really known. But one day out of the blue, Dad decided he wanted me to have a mom. Apparently, I needed a female caregiver and role model, and just like that he married my stepmom, and Mom got packed up and put in the basement.

I would sneak down there whenever I had the chance and go through her things. You can learn a lot about a person by snooping through their belongings and I wanted to know everything about her. When I moved out to go to college, I snuck a box out. I put all of my favorite things, things that made me feel close to her, in it. Going through the box now, I smile at the familiar items. I open my photo album and stare at the pictures of my mom holding me as a baby. She's so beautiful and even in a picture, I still get lost in her eyes. Something in her calls to me. Demanding I see *something*. I just wish I knew what the hell I was supposed to be looking for.

She has long brown, almost black, hair swept up in some gorgeous, effortless up-do that probably actually took a lot of time to perfect. She looks like she should be on billboards advertising skincare products, she never wore make-up, but her skin glowed. I don't know if it was just good genes or the sheer joy and love radiating from her that made her look so stunning. Feeling that nagging sensation that I'm missing something, I study the picture more closely. Even as a baby, I looked a lot like her. I for sure got my smooth alabaster skin from her, my dad's much more tan than we are.

My eyes skip from feature to feature, mentally comparing us. I finally get to her eyes and pause. They're so dark they're almost black… maybe they *are* black. Setting the book beside me on the couch, I turn my camera on and stare at my eyes, trying to discern what color they are. They look more hazel to me, but the longer I stare, the more they dilate, which is not helping. Hoping I have some pictures that show them clearly, I flip through my gallery, stopping on a picture of me and my dad. It was my birthday and we went out just the two of us. It was so great to spend time with him without my stepmom trying to weasel her way in. We're both laughing and our entire faces are lit from within. For once, my eyes are open, they typically close when I'm laughing, so I zoom in to see them better.

I always thought my eyes were a rich brown, but looking at them now, they're definitely more black, like Dad's coffee. I guess my eyes change colors... How have I not noticed that before? Holding the two pictures next to each other, it's startling how much I look like her. It's not obvious, but when you look at us side by side the similarities stand out. We could be sisters... I mean if she looked like this *now* that is. I'm sure she's aged though, wherever the hell she is.

As I compare the pictures, my eyes are drawn to her necklace. I've always found it fascinating. It has this stone that I swear doesn't exist. I've never seen anything like it, and trust me, I've looked everywhere. It's oval-shaped and set in this delicate metal cage. The stone is smooth and a radiant transparent blue... like blue flames. The swirling metal encasing it is a deep black that seems to completely absorb all the light.

Setting my phone and the photo album down, I reach into the box and pull out the necklace. I always wanted to wear it, to feel closer to her, but the chain is broken and I was too afraid to mess with it and potentially make matters worse. It would be my luck that I would break the amulet too. Holding the stone in my hand, I could swear the blue flickers then flares even brighter and it starts to grow warm in my hand. I drop it in shock when it burns me. Looking at my palm, I see what looks like a symbol burned onto my skin. Before my eyes though, it simply disappears like it was never there. If I would have blinked I might have missed it.

Running my finger over the spot, I'm perplexed by the lack of a mark. I know I wasn't imagining it.

"How did you summon me?" A quiet voice questions, he doesn't seem mad, just curious.

I snap my head up at the question. Somehow I managed to summon yet another fucking demon. Wait... "Zephyr?" How the fuck did I summon *him*? The demon tilts his head and scrutinizes me and I'm getting more and more confused by the second.

"No. How did you summon me? And how do you know my brother?"

"Brother? Oh my God, you're Z's brother?" At his raised brow and impatient look, I give in a little. "I accidentally summoned him the other day." I shrug like it's no big deal, I totally summon demons all the time... which, I guess I kinda *do*. His glare tells me that wasn't enough information for him, but it's all he's gonna get so he better get over it.

"Is there a reason you're not telling me how you were able to summon me?"

Well, I don't know how I ever thought this asshole was Zephyr. Yeah, they look alike, but they don't talk or act the same at all. This guy has a cool, aloof exterior. He's very alert, covertly scanning the room, looking for who knows what. And he has this calm, yet commanding, soft voice. He looks slightly agitated that I'm not answering him, but he's just waiting me out. Any other guy would have gotten pissed and started yelling by now. I'm intrigued by him, so I decide to finally tell him what I was doing before he popped in. His eyes widen when I tell him about the necklace and he holds his hand out to me.

"Let me see it," he commands. At my raised brow he sighs. "Please," he quietly amends.

Rolling my eyes, I bend over and pick the necklace off the floor, holding it up for him to see. Before I realize what's happening he's taken it from my hand. I watch with narrowed eyes as he inspects it, noticing every minute twitch on his face.

"Where did you get this?"

"Okay, you're cute, but your conversation skills need some work," I grumble.

"My apologies. I am not like my brother. I don't get *summoned*," he sneers the word and now I really want to know what that's about.

"Oh, well there's a first time for everything. What are the odds that I would summon *two* non-summonable demons in one week?" I muse to myself. Of course, he hears, because the demon doesn't miss anything.

"Who else have you summoned?"

I glare at him, but I have a feeling I'm going to have to get used to his concise way of speaking. "If you must know, I summoned Belzar, too." I cross my arms, arching my brow in challenge. "Actually, where the hell *is* Belzar? I've tried summoning him a million times. I'm worried about him. He said he was going to work to talk to his boss about the... uhhh never mind, he just... he said he was going to work, but he'd come back when I summoned him. But it didn't work."

"So you're the girl... I can see why they'd be infatuated with you," he murmurs, slowly nodding as he runs his gaze over me.

A shiver races through my body and I have a flash of him naked, hovering over me in bed, whispering dirty, dirty things in his no-nonsense way. I feel my face heat at the unbidden mental image and quickly turn my head so he doesn't see. Should have known better.

"Why is your face doing that? Are you warm? Don't you have air conditioning?" he asks as he looks around the room.

"I'm fine. Shut up," I grumble. "We were talking about Belz, remember? Where is he?"

"Well, you said he was going to work, so I imagine that's where he is."

Ugh, this guy, I swear, men are so dumb sometimes.

"Fine, he's at work. Where's Zephyr? Last I heard he was going to the outskirts, but Belz sounded like that was a big deal, so I'm worried about him too."

"He went to the outskirts? Why?" He actually sounds a little worried at that news.

"I don't know. Find him and ask him yourself," I snap. I'm pretty tired of this one-way conversation. I ask questions and get bupkis, but he expects detailed answers anytime he asks me anything. Fuck that shit. I deserve answers too.

"I'm not done with my questions. You still haven't told me where you got this necklace." He dangles said necklace in front of him and I snatch it out of his hand.

"Well, too damn bad. Once you can tell me Belz and Zeph are okay, I'll tell you all about the necklace. Until then, I'm done with your stupid questions."

"Fine. I'll find *our* lover and my brother. If you need me, do whatever you were doing with the pendent before I got here," he instructs. After I acquiesce, he pops out in a cloud of smoke and I'm alone once again.

SIXTEEN

ZARRETH

The girl is intriguing, I'll give her that. If she didn't seem so genuinely concerned about Zeph and Belz, I would have stuck around and made her tell me where she got that fucking amulet; *I* made that fucking necklace and it *should be* in Gehenna with its owner. Instead, I head home, checking to see if my idiot brother is back yet. I search the entire house and come up empty. No one is here, not even Fireball. I hope that means the fuckhead took the hound with him. I swear I don't know what the hell goes on in his fucking head sometimes.

I take off to the gate, hoping to run into him on his way home. When I get there I see Sonnoz manning the gate.

"Hey, Sonnoz. You seen Zephyr lately?" I call as I approach him.

"Zarreth. Nah, man, I haven't seen him since he left this morning," he offers with a shrug.

"You know where he went?"

"Just said he was after some low-life. I didn't ask too many questions. He looked like he was in a hurry and that hound of yours looked like he was about to eat me."

I can't hold back the smirk at that. Dumbass probably said the wrong thing and Fireball *was* in fact about to eat him. Zeph probably saved his life.

"You see him, tell him I'm looking for him. I'm headed to the castle. Tell the fucker to come find me," I order, then spin around and start walking before he can utter his assurances. I'm about to kill two birds with one stone; find Belz and determine what the fuck is going on, *and* learn how that fucking girl has that damn amulet.

It's times like now I wish I had wings like Belzar. I understand the castle has to be far away from the gate for security purposes, but fuck it's a long walk. Not helped by the fact that it's quitting time and the streets are filled with demons trying to get home. I slip through the mass of demons unperturbed. I may not *like* crowds, but I was made to infiltrate them and learn their secrets without anyone ever suspecting a thing. I pick up bits and pieces of conversation as I go, filing away what sticks out to investigate later. By the time I reach the castle, I have a list of things to dig into in the morning, but first I have questions and I'm not leaving here without answers.

The guard sees my 'don't fuck with me' demeanor and immediately opens the door. I take the hallway to the right and follow it to my destination. She's not going to be happy to see me, but it can't be helped, so she can get the fuck over it. I rap on the purple door and politely wait for it to open.

"Zar? What are you-" Belz starts, before I push past him into the room. I haven't been welcome in this place for a long time, but it looks just like I remember.

"Belzar, who is it? You know I don't like… *You*," she sneers when she sees me. "What are you doing here? You know you're not welcome in my presence." She rises from her chair and looks like she's about to attack me if I don't get gone *now*. Too bad for her that's not going to happen.

"Shut up and sit down. I have some questions for you, and you're damn well going to answer them," I order the fucking princess of Hell like she couldn't incinerate me where I stand.

Too speechless from my unexpected display, she stands there with her mouth agape.

"Zar, what the fuck man?"

"I'll get to you." I glare at him in return.

"Care to explain to me, how this chick that's apparently sleeping with this ass *and* my brother, has the fucking amulet I made for *you?* When you came back you wouldn't tell me *anything*. After everything I fucking did for you back then, you just locked me out. As if I didn't deserve to know. I put my fucking neck on the line for you, Zofina! And this is how you repay me. Years of childish animosity. Refusing to *look* at me, much less *speak* to me. Well, it's fucking *done*. I want answers. Where were you? Why'd you come back? Who is this girl that has your amulet?"

"Wait, you saw Maddy? *How?*" Belz is the first to speak.

"Yes, I saw your girlfriend. And I don't know how. Apparently, she has a knack for accidentally summoning demons. She said she was worried about you because she's tried summoning you and you're obviously not coming. *Then* she told me my idiot brother went to the outskirts. What the fuck is that about?"

"What do you mean she's been summoning me? How am I not there then? You can't resist a summons."

"Remember I told you my father made it so I couldn't leave again? It's the castle, Belz. Summons can't breach the barrier he put over it. As long as you're in the castle, you can't be summoned," the princess explains.

"Well, that answers *that* question. Since you're obviously capable, let's get to my fucking questions now," I snap. I'm getting rather impatient. Something is going on here and I don't like being out of the loop.

The princess sighs and sits back in her wingback chair. It's purple velvet and she's had it for as long as I can remember.

"Madelyne is my daughter. When you helped me escape…" She has the decency to grimace at that. "I found my mate. We fell madly in love and settled down. We had Maddy and everything was perfect. Until the day she pulled a little too hard on my chain and broke it. I knew with the chain broken it would send an alert to you, and father would send someone to get me. I didn't want to risk their lives, so I came back on my own. I left the amulet. I guess Maddy kept it." She finishes with a tear in her eye.

I can see the resemblance now as I stare at the princess. It's not obvious and is somewhat difficult to compare the two because Madelyne is human, and Zofina is in her demon form now, but it's there. "Does anyone else know this?" I ask as calmly as I can.

"No. I haven't told a soul until today. When Belzar told me that she was-" She cuts herself off and now I'm interested to know just what she *is* to Belzar.

"Oh no. Don't stop there, Princess. I want to know everything."

"It's not my story to tell, Zarreth. If Belzar wants you to know, he can tell you."

Fucking Hell. What the fuck is going on? I run my hand over my face, then rub my temples trying to calm down. Belzar can be a fucking vault when he wants to be. If I start demanding shit from him, it won't get me far. I'm surprised when he speaks up.

"What did you think of her? Were you mean to her?

Did you…" he sighs and scratches the back of his head. "Did you *feel* anything when you met her?"

"She's intriguing. I don't believe I was mean to her, maybe a little short, but not outright antagonistic. And what do you mean did I *feel* anything?"

"Why do you say she's intriguing?" He latches onto that instead of answering my fucking question because of course, he does.

"I don't know, there's just something about her that speaks to me. I can see why you and Zeph are bewitched by her." What the fuck is he getting at? The two of them share a look and when the princess nods, Belz sighs even heavier than before.

"Maddy is our mate. I had no clue she was Zo's daughter. I came to her to get more information about mates."

Mate? She's his fucking *mate?* Wait did he say *our.* "She's *whose* mate?"

"Mine, Zephyr's, I'm willing to bet *yours.* Hell, I wouldn't be surprised if she was fucking Oz's mate at this fucking rate," he grumbles.

"Now, hold the fuck on here. Why the Hell do you think she's *my* mate? I don't want and I don't *need* a fucking mate. No fucking thank you."

"I felt a pull to her the moment I laid eyes on her. You say she's intriguing, but you don't really know why or how. Something pulls you to her, just like it did me. I think that's the mate bond calling you," he says.

"Has anyone ever had that many mates?" Why am I even entertaining this idea?

"No. Only my father has ever had more than one."

Well, *fuck.* I don't know what it could mean that she has so many mates... *If* she has that many, but it can't be good.

"What was Zeph doing in the outskirts?" I question Belz.

"Fuck! He was looking for *Chad,*" he snarls.

"Who the fuck is Chad? And why are you so pissed right now?" I tilt my head, trying to put the pieces together, but I'm clearly missing something vital to this puzzle.

"*Chad* is a low-level demon scum that's after Maddy. I couldn't figure out why he would have any interest in her, but *now* I think the answer to that is obvious. He *knows.* He has to. I don't know what the hell he's planning on doing with her, but he's under the illusion that she's his. I tried to scare him off, but he doubled down. He showed up at her work in fucking demon form. If she hadn't summoned Zephyr and me in time, I don't know what would have happened to her. Fuck! Someone has to get back to her. I don't want her to be alone until we know where he is and what he's planning. Hell, I don't want her to be alone ever again."

"You left my baby girl *alone* when you knew there was a demon after her?! Are you out of your fucking mind? What the hell is wrong with you two? So help me... If anything happens to her Belzar, I'm holding you personally responsible. Do you understand me?" Zofina goes off on Belz.

"Yes, Zo, I understand. I don't know how I'm going to get to her though. I can only leave if I'm summoned. I may have to just go home and wait for her to summon me again," he groans.

"Just get out of this castle and you'll be there. The summoning she's already done will take you once it can get a hold of you. Just… keep her safe Belzar. Please."

I've never seen the princess look so vulnerable; like she may fall apart at any moment. Belz hugs her, then dashes out of the room before I can say anything. Instead of running after him, I turn to the princess.

"Is that why you've been avoiding and ignoring me all these years? You thought I would turn on you when the beacon came in, and you've been holding it against me? Even though it didn't even happen?"

"I don't know, Zarreth. I guess so." She shrugs like the past twenty-five years haven't been hell for me because of her.

"You know the worst part about that? When the beacon did come in, I silenced it. I didn't alert the guard. No one knew. You could have stayed because *I* kept your fucking secret. Then you came back, pissed at the world, and took it out on me. But you know what? You weren't the only one, Zofina. Lucifer came to see me after you got back. He wanted to know why I didn't know where you were, that you were coming home. Imagine his surprise when I told him I turned off your beacon." I pause, taking a small breath, before continuing.

"You thought I would betray *you,* but really I betrayed him. I didn't go unpunished for my crimes either. Or did you never wonder why I was gone for so long? Hell, you probably didn't even realize it. He locked me up, Zo. He punished me *himself.* Know how many demons can say the devil himself met out their penance?" I reveal my deepest secret. No one knows where I was. I told the guys I was on a mission. This is the first time I've spoken the words.

"Oh, Zarreth! I'm so sorry. I had no idea. I didn't... I didn't tell him you helped me. No matter how mad I was because of my misguided assumption. Are you... are you okay?"

"I'm fine. Now, if you'll excuse me, I'm going home. And staying far away from your daughter. She sounds like trouble." With that, I turn and walk out of the room that used to be so familiar to me, for the last time. I wish Zephyr and Belz the best, but I want no part of this mess. I don't care how attractive she is.

SEVENTEEN

BELZAR

I take off down the hall, not waiting for Zar. I've got a feeling he's got some things he needs to get off his chest when it comes to Zofina anyway. He may be a while and I don't have time to waste. Turning the corner, I barrel through the door, sending the guard flying. As soon as I take two steps away from the castle entrance I feel like I'm being ripped apart, the pull is so strong. I try to breathe through the sensation as I manifest in Maddy's living room.

Expecting Maddy to launch herself at me when the smoke dissipates, I'm surprised to find the room empty.

"Maddy? Maddy, where are you?" I call, as I start walking around the apartment looking for her.

I check the kitchen first then move down the hallway,

looking in the bathroom, then the bedroom, but there's no sign of her. She's not here. I walk back to the living room, hoping she left a note or something in case I magically showed up while she was gone. That's when I finally notice the state of the room. There was clearly a struggle, the lamp is knocked over, the tables are askew, and there's a box on the floor with its contents spilling out.

Approaching the couch, I examine the scene more closely, looking for some clue as to what the fuck happened here. There's a puddle of orange liquid and glasses strewn all over the table and floor. Bending down, I pick up a black chain that looks familiar. Studying the chain, I realize it's made from spiatrium; a metal only found in remote parts of Hell. It's very rare, but not exactly strong, hence the broken chain. This necklace is missing something though. There's a delicate cage attached to the chain, but there should be something *in* the cage. Whatever it is, it's gone now.

My blood boils when my eyes roam over the scene and land on a splatter of blood. Swiping my finger through it, I bring it to my nose, inhaling the sweet scent of my mate. Sticking out my tongue, I lick the blood from my finger, going deadly still when I'm hit with the fear she was feeling when she spilled it. I will find whoever did this and kill them if it's the last thing I do.

Taking a deep breath, I sit on her couch, trying to center myself. I must do this right, there's no room for error, so I focus entirely on Maddy. Until my only thought is her. My whole being buzzes with the need to find her. To bring her back to me. I picture her in my head, concentrating until I can see every detail as if she were standing right in front of me. I feel like I could reach out and touch her. Wherever she is, she looks *pissed*. Not that I can blame her. I'm shocked when she starts talking, but I'm quick to focus before I lose her.

"I don't know what you think you're doing, *Chad,* but it's not going to work. I'm not *yours.* I never will be. Get it through your ugly ass head!" she screeches.

Fuck. He does have her. I've gotta call the guys. I don't care if Zarreth wants to be her mate or not, he'll help me find her. He's the best man for the job. He can find her. No matter where she is.

"Don't worry, *Amica Mea.* I'm coming for you. I'll get you back," I whisper.

Before I disconnect, I see her looking around the room with her brows furrowed. "Belz?"

Shit, she heard me.

"Belz can't save you now, Maddy. He'll never find you. Well… not until it's too late anyway," he taunts, then does some stupid wannabe evil villain laugh.

"Don't listen to him, baby. I'll always find you. Just stay safe. We're coming," I vow, cutting our connection before I give in to my need to stay with her. I can't hold the connection for long and I have to summon the guys. The sooner I get them all here, the sooner I have her in my arms again.

Flipping my hand over, I slice the fleshy part of my palm with my nail, cupping my hand for the blood to pool in my palm. I dip my finger in the blood and lean over to draw an intricate symbol onto the table. By the time I finish the last precise line, the cut has healed and I'm left with dry blood on my hands. Clouds of smoke start popping up all over the room and I slump against the back of the couch, worn out from the amount of energy it took to summon all of them at the same time.

"Where the *fuck* am I?!"

"Belzar! Why the fuck did you bring me here?"

"What's happening? Where's Maddy? Why are they here?"

The three of them all talk at once as soon as the smoke clears. Groggily, I attempt to raise a hand to get them to shut the fuck up, but it falls limply to my lap when I get it chest high. Taking a deep breath, I try to recover enough to explain to them what the fuck is going on.

"Belz? Are you okay? What's wrong?" Zephyr rushes over to me, dropping to his knees and running his hands all over me as if looking for a wound.

"I'm… fine," I get out, but I'm feeling light-headed. "He took her, Zeph. I don't know... how long, but she's gone." His eyes widen at my breathless confession but I need to tell him the rest of it. "I saw her. She looked…" Fucking hell. It would be nice if I could fucking talk without having to stop to catch my damn breath. "Roughed up, but she was her typical snarky self. She called him out by name. That's how I know it's him."

"Son of a bitch! How did he fucking get her? Belz, we *have* to get her back." He's not handling this well, and I'm too fucking weak to do anything about it. Thankfully, for once, Oz steps up.

"Hey, it's okay, Z. I don't know why she's so damn important to you two, but we'll help. We'll find her and get her back to you," he vows, giving Zar a look that says 'you better fucking help or I'll kill you myself.'

"Of course we'll help," Zar agrees, rolling his eyes.

"Good. Process the room. We need to know everything that happened here," Oz seamlessly takes charge of the situation, Zarreth taking off to do just that, starting at the front door where it's assumed the fuckface came in.

"Fuck! I have to tell Zo. She's gonna freak out," I groan.

"Zo? Why the hell would you have to tell her about this?" Oz asks with his arms crossed and brows furrowed.

Scrubbing my hand down my face, I inform him. "Because she's her *mother*."

Zeph stares at me with wide eyes and Oz drops his arms muttering, "Shiiiit."

That about sums it up.

"I'll tell her. Does she know about…" Zeph trails off.

"Yeah. I told her."

"Does she know what? What the fuck is going on?" Oz grumbles.

Zeph and I share a look and I sigh, nodding my head. "Maddy is our mate." Fuck Oz was the only one that didn't know, might as well tell him.

"Your?" He points between us with solid black eyes. "*Mate*," he grinds out between clenched teeth.

At the pure malice in his tone, Zeph grimaces then slowly turns to face our pissed-off lover. "It doesn't mean…" he starts before Oz cuts him off with a glare. "Oh stop. It doesn't! She knows about us. She wouldn't make us stop seeing you. If that happens it'll be because *you* decided, not her."

"Whatever. We'll just fucking see, won't we? Go tell your new mother-in-law that her long-lost daughter is missing. We'll summon you back when we have some idea what to fucking do."

Zeph turns to me in question. I can see how worried he is so I try to project a sense of calm and determination when I tell him, "Go. We'll find her."

Nodding once, he stands and kisses me before turning, grabbing Oz by the shirt and pulling him in for a scorching kiss that makes *my* dick twitch, before disappearing in a cloud of smoke.

EIGHTEEN

ZOFINA

I've been pacing my room like a caged animal since Zarreth left. I can't believe I thought the worst of him. This whole time I've been secretly blaming him for me being here, away from my mate and my baby. When really it's *my* fault. If I would have just had some faith in him, I could have watched Madelyne grow up. I could be a part of her life right now. But I was so sure Father would find me and take them from me. I couldn't risk it, couldn't risk *them.* What good did coming home do? Yeah, they're alive, but I missed out on so much. Not to mention the hell Zar went through because of me. And all this time... he never said a word. He just let me go on hating him when he should have been the one hating *me.*

Knowing that Madelyne has grown into a beautiful

woman and that my very best friends are her mates... I *have* to find a way out of here. I have to see her. Explain why I left the way I did. I just hope it's not too late. Belz said someone was after her. I need to talk to Zephyr, see who this demon is. As I have the thought, the demon bursts through my door, panting like he ran here.

"Zofina!" he gasps as he stops in front of me.

"Zephyr? What's the matter?" I grab his hand, backing away with my own gasp when I look into his desolate eyes. "What happened?"

"It's Maddy. She's gone."

"Gone? What do you mean *gone*? Zephyr, I need you to pull yourself together and tell me what the hell is going on," I order.

Taking a deep breath, he starts again. "Chad took her. When Belz got to her apartment, there were signs of a struggle and her blood was on the table. He summoned us and told us what happened. I volunteered to come tell you. I thought you'd want to know." By the time he finishes his story, he looks like he's on the verge of a panic attack.

"You did the right thing. I may have killed you all had you not told me," I mumble under my breath. If my daughter was kidnapped and no one told me about it, there would be hell to pay.

I start pacing again as my mind spins with possibilities. What is he doing to her? How are we going to find her? I have to go. I have to find her. I can't stay locked up in this God-forsaken castle while my baby is in the hands of some lunatic. I can't rely on anyone else to find her. Even if I know they would do absolutely anything for my daughter, and they're the best at what they do. If anyone could find her it would be those four. But I just can't sit on the sidelines anymore.

"I'm going to my father," I state with a determined countenance.

"I... uh... I don't have to come with you, do I?" he stutters.

"No. Go back to the others. I'll be there shortly." One way or another I'm leaving Hell tonight.

I find my father in his favorite torture chamber. It's where he prefers to spend his free time, inflicting as much torment as he can on anyone who incurs his wrath. Today's guest is currently strapped to a St. Andrews Cross with blood pouring down his back. The flesh has been torn apart so badly I don't think there's a single spot on him that is not cut up. This does not deter Father any. He continues raining the cat-o'-nine-tails down on him, each razor-sharp end slicing into him over and over.

"Did you need something, Daughter?" he calls in a sickeningly sweet voice, not missing a beat as he flicks his hand, sending the whip to the demon's leg causing him to cry out at the unexpected pain. Idiot. Father lives for the cries, the wails, the whimpers. He soaks up every sound.

"I need to discuss something important with you. Could you pause your torture for a moment? Maybe give him time to catch his breath so he can scream for you when you resume?" I suggest.

"A marvelous idea, Daughter. Perhaps you'll join me when we've finished our talk." He looks so hopeful it pains me to turn him down for once.

In response, I straighten my spine even more than it already was-if that's possible-spin on my heels and walk out the door, my father's booming chuckle following in my wake. This is going to be a difficult conversation, and I definitely don't want him anywhere near torture devices. I would much prefer he not turn that whip on me, thank you very much. Walking down the hall, I turn into his office and pace the room while I wait for him to catch up and close the door.

"Now, what's this all about? You never want to talk to me," he all but whines, as he sits in his high back wing chair. It's exactly like mine, except for black where mine is purple.

"Some things have been brought to my attention and I think it's time you know the truth." Fuck I thought this was going to be easier, but I may wear a hole in his rug with all of my pacing.

"And which truth is that, my dear?" He leans back in his chair, crossing his foot over one knee, holding his ankle with one hand and tapping his knee with the fingers of his other hand, as he watches me pace back and forth in front of him.

"The truth about why I left and what happened while I was gone," I declare, getting a tiny bit of enjoyment out of it when his beat stutters before starting again. It's the only outward indication that my announcement affects him in any way.

"Please, be my guest," he offers with a wave of his hand. "I've been waiting for this for a very long time. But I'm a patient man, darling. I gave you your time and space, all the while awaiting the day you would come to me. You have my undivided attention, Daughter."

Just rip the bandaid off. It won't be that bad. Madelyne is counting on you. "When I left…" I start, but he cuts me off.

"Ah ah ah. You said you'd tell me *why* you left. Start there."

Ugh. Fine, I'll start there, but you're not going to like it. "I left because I was so sick of Majorkorie constantly bitching. She did nothing but complain about how I had it so easy here. That I was the favorite. She went out of her way to make my life miserable. I couldn't take it anymore, I had to get away. So I did. I wasn't planning on staying gone. I had every intention of coming home, but then I met my mate. He was everything I never wanted. He made me feel things I didn't know I could feel. I couldn't give that up."

"You left because of *Majorkorie*?" His once jovial voice turns to ice and I take a healthy step back.

"Y-yes," I stutter. Even I'm not stupid enough to not be scared of him when he uses that tone.

He takes a calming breath before addressing me again. "You know she was telling the truth. You *are* my favorite. You always have been. That's why it hurt me so much when you left without even telling me."

I'm shocked by the admission. Not that I'm his favorite, I've known that. We've always had a very close relationship. But that he would admit it out loud.

"I will deal with Majorkorie. You know, now that I'm thinking about the wretched girl, I don't think I've seen her in some time." He sits forward, waking up his computer and typing away. "I've sent word to security to determine her whereabouts. I can't even recall when the last time I saw her was." He rubs his chin while he thinks about it.

"I wouldn't know, honestly. I've hardly left my room since I've been home. Have never left the castle. I think I may have seen her once or twice in all the years since I've been home," I admit.

"She is my least favorite child, so I have not kept track of her. Obviously, that was an oversight on my behalf. Please, go on with your story. Your sister will be duly punished once she is found." The ice is still in his voice, but only when he mentions Marjorkorie.

Taking a deep breath, I prepare myself for the next part

of the story. I tell him about Madelyne. How perfect she was, how much I loved her. I finish my story by telling him why I returned home and how heartbroken and miserable I've been since I came back. The entire time, he's staring at me with unseeing eyes, like he's seeing right through me.

"You have a daughter." It's not a question, but I nod regardless. "You left your mate and your infant because you thought I would send someone to kill them? You think so lowly of me? Why would I not welcome your mate and your child with open arms? They are yours, Zofina. Therefore they are mine. I would have treasured your beloved."

What? What is he saying? "But… no. No." I shake my head repeatedly in utter denial that I could have been so wrong about everything. About Zarreth. About Father. Surely he doesn't mean…

"Of course, I mean it, Zofina. You should have told me. We could have saved ourselves a lot of heartache if I had just known. I would have asked to meet them. To have a chance to be a part of my granddaughter's life." He pauses as the thought hits home. "My *granddaughter.* Where is she? I want to meet her. And your mate."

"That's why I told you about her. She's missing. Someone found out about her. A low-level demon kidnapped her tonight. I have to leave, Father. I need to find her before it's too late." A chill runs down my spine thinking about what he could be doing to her right now, but I steel my resolve to find her and end their lives. It will be slow and painful.

"How do you know this if you have not seen her since your return home?" he questions. It's a valid question since I left out the bit about Belzar and Zephyr.

"I would know nothing of her life right now if she hadn't accidentally summoned Belzar," I tell him.

"Belzar? Why would she summon him? *How* did she summon him? He has never been summoned before."

"It appears she's rather adept at unintentionally summoning demons," I offer with a smile and a shrug. "She has called not just Belzar, but Zephyr and Zarreth as well. It appears they're her mates. Well, we know for sure Belzar and Zephyr are. Zarreth only just met her and I don't believe she's had the pleasure of meeting Oz yet."

I don't believe I've ever seen my father look so surprised.

"*Four* mates. She must be very powerful indeed. And each of them strong, impressive demons in their own right. You know I always wanted you to be with Zarreth," he muses.

"Yes, I might recall something like that." I smirk as I shake my head. Father was relentless in trying to push us together. It worked, we were extremely close, though never in the way Father had wished. Now I'm thankful we never went beyond a great friendship. It would be extremely awkward to have slept with your daughter's mate.

"Now, I'm assuming they're on Earth searching for her?"

"Of course. Zephyr came to tell me what happened. I told him to go back and help them and I would be there after I spoke with you."

"You know I can't come with you." He frowns at the thought. As if it pains him that he has to stay here while someone else searches for his granddaughter that he's never even met. "I will unlock your powers. You will be able to find her easily since you share blood. I might suggest you go to the boys first. They would likely not be happy about being left out."

"Thank you, Father. I will bring them with me. I couldn't leave her mates out."

"Good. Capture the demon that's responsible and bring him here. I will have my torture chamber cleaned for you."

If I thought the ice in his tone when talking about Marjorkorie was bad, it has nothing on the vehemence with which he delivers that order. It most assuredly *is* an order. I have no doubt he will let me and Madelyne's mates torture the vermin, but he will have his pound of flesh too. I simply nod once then make my way to the door. I've wasted enough time talking, now it's time for action.

NINETEEN

MADELYNE

How do I keep summoning all these damn demons? I'm not trying to, at least the first time. I'm *definitely* trying to summon Belz now. I wish I knew why he wasn't coming. Is he hurt? God, I can't even think that. I'll for sure have a panic attack if I think of either of them dead in some Hell ditch somewhere. Deciding I need to take a break and clear my head, I go to my room and grab my comfy pjs. I think a bath is in order.

Turning the tub on, I drop in my favorite bath bomb, it has a soft scent of sweet vanilla, real marshmallow powder, and just a hint of soothing lavender. It always relaxes me even as it makes me crave something sweet. Maybe if I smell good enough to eat when my guys finally get here, they'll do just that. I could go for a tag team night. But this time, I'll have both of them. It made me sad that I fell asleep before I was able to take them both last night, but the whole mate thing really threw us through a loop. I'm pretty happy with the way it ended though. I slept amazingly curled up between the two of them. I've never felt more safe and cherished in my entire life.

Sinking into the foamy water, I lean back against the wall, closing my eyes as I recall last night. Zeph was something else. I've never had a man pay so much attention to my every minute reaction. Well, except for Belz obviously. I wonder if it's a demon thing or a mate thing. Either way, I can definitely get used to it. They make my body sing in a way I never thought possible.

Thinking about it, I can't help my hand trailing down my body to find my needy clit. Rubbing slow circles around the bud, I remember what it felt like to have two tongues fighting over it. I don't think I've ever experienced something so fucking sexy in my life. Though I've got a feeling things will only get hotter with them. My mind turns to all the ways I can have both of them at the same time; taking turns sucking their cocks, riding Belz while Zeph fucks my face, riding Zeph while Belz fucks my ass. Oh, God. I'm so fucking turned on just thinking about it. I wish they were here to make my fantasies a reality.

I'm so fucking keyed up, my fingers aren't doing it for me anymore, so I move to a jet. Getting on my knees and holding onto the side of the tub, I'm reminded of my first time in it. I'm learning Belz doesn't half-ass anything. He's always extremely thorough when it comes to my pleasure and making sure he's always on my mind. He knew doing that, I'd always think of him whenever I even *look* at a tub.

The jet isn't nearly as much fun without Belz's cock slamming into me from behind, or his deep voice telling me to come for him. But it does the job, getting me off when my fingers aren't up to snuff. I remember something else Belz said to me while he was fucking me against this jet. Something that sends a thrill through me at the idea. He said I would get off by him and with his permission. I wonder if he'll punish me when I tell him what I did. If he ever fucking shows up.

Draining the tub, I get out, dry off and slip into my comfy clothes. As I'm drying my hair, I hear a noise from the kitchen. It's about fucking time! I walk out and head that way, ready to give the demon a piece of my mind, but stop in my tracks when I see it's not the demon I was expecting. How the hell did Chad get in my apartment? He's in his human form, so hopefully, that means he's not here to hurt me. I have nothing to defend myself with, so I think of the next best thing.

Zarreth said I could summon him with Mom's necklace, so I make a dash for the living room hoping he doesn't see me until I can summon Zarreth. As soon as I make it to the room, he speaks from behind me, giving me chills.

"Maddy. I've been waiting for you," he says, voice dripping poisoned sugar.

I don't even look back at him, I reach out and grab the chain off the table. When I stand up, I can feel him behind me.

"What's this, Maddy? A little souvenir from Mommy? Something to remind you of the bitch that left you?" he taunts me, his warm breath blowing on my neck and cheek.

At his vile words, I turn and smack him across the face. "Don't you fucking talk about my mother like that you piece of shit!"

His eyes turn that milky white and he slowly starts to shift more and more into his demon form.

"That was very stupid, Maddy," he snarls with his pointy fucking teeth.

Without warning, he backhands me, and I go flying onto the coffee table, knocking glasses over, spilling the Dreamsicles I made to summon Belz. Rolling off the table, I reach out a hand to pull myself up. Only succeeding in knocking the box off the couch. Motherfucker! He's going to pay for that. Finally, I stand up and turn to face him. He's fully in demon form now and somehow looks even uglier than I remember.

"Man, how are you so fucking ugly? It never ceases to

amaze me how different you look as a demon. It really sucks being a low-level scum doesn't it?" Why am I antagonizing a demon that broke into my house in the middle of the night and clearly doesn't have good intentions for me? No idea, I'm just that kind of smart, what can I say?

This time, instead of hitting *me,* he swings his grotesque hand, smashing my lamp to the floor.

"Enough! Shut your stupid mouth and come with me of your own volition, or I'll *take* you and it won't be fun for you," he growls the ultimatum.

"If you think I'm going anywhere with you, you're stupider than I thought."

"Good. I was hoping you'd choose the hard way." He smiles and I can see every one of his monstrous teeth as he approaches me.

I take a step back as I rub the fucking amulet, cursing Zarreth for not fucking showing up already. Chad zeroes in on the necklace in my hand. I was trying to be stealthy, but he caught on because his eyes snag on my hands then flick back up to my eyes.

"What are you doing with that? It's not just a reminder of Mommy, is it?" He reaches out, trying to snatch it from my hands, but I'm not letting go without a fight.

I stomp on his foot, causing him to howl and release the chain for a moment before looking at me with murder in his dead eyes. Faster than I can see, he grabs the necklace and pulls it from my grip, breaking the delicate cage, and unknowingly leaving the stone in my hand. He holds up the chain between us and taunts me with it. Not wanting him to realize I have the piece I want, I make a grab for it, but he hits me again.

This time when I go down, I slip the stone in my pocket. I don't know what he wants with me, but it's clear he's not leaving without me. Maybe the stone will come in handy.

"Get up. We need to get to your new home before my partner gets there. I can't wait to introduce you to your aunt. It'll be a fun family reunion," he smirks.

My aunt*? What the fuck is he talking about?* Guess I'll find out soon because he's dragging me up and in seconds a cloud of smoke surrounds us.

When the smoke clears, I'm surprised to see we're in a house. A crappy, run-down house, but a house nonetheless. I look around, cataloging my surroundings. Searching for a way out, something to use as a weapon, literally anything that could possibly help me at some point. I may have been kidnapped and am now being held against my will, but I'm no damsel in distress. I'll bide my time then kick this fucker's ass myself and get the fuck out of here. I won't be the 'woe is me', helpless girl, just waiting for a strong man to save me.

"Now, while we wait, let's get a few things out of the way."

I snap my head around to see Chad back in his human form. Goody. At least I don't have to look at his ugly face.

"Mar-*my partner* has graciously granted me your hand and all of the *perks* that go with marrying you."

"Jesus Christ! I'm not fucking marrying you, you freak! And your *partner* can fuck herself."

"You *are* mine, Maddy. It's time you realize the inevitable. We'll just stay in this lovely house until you accept the facts. Come on, I'll show you to our room."

He grabs my arm and drags me down the hall, stopping at a pristine white door that's out of place in this dump of a house. He smiles his most charming smile as he opens the door, walking in, and pulling me behind him. I look around and the room is gorgeous. The entire space is pristine, from the freshly painted walls and ceiling to the refinished hardwood floors. The white four-poster bed in the middle of the room is draped in sheer curtains. I briefly wonder if he has the power to create things like Belz does, but I'm sure that's an upper-level demon trait. Surely he can't do that. Under any other circumstance, I would *love* this room. It's too bad it's in this dilapidated house and Chad is acting like this is *our* room.

"I don't know what you think you're doing, *Chad,* but it's not going to work. I'm not *yours.* I never will be. Get it through your ugly ass head!" I screech.

"Don't worry, Amica Mea. *I'm coming for you. I'll get you back."* The words are ghosted by my ear and I look around trying to find the source.

"Belz?" I whisper in disbelief.

"Belz can't save you now, Maddy. He'll never find you. Well... not until it's too late anyway," Chad taunts, then does some stupid wannabe evil villain laugh.

"Don't listen to him, baby. I'll always find you. Just stay safe. We're coming," the voice says before it goes silent.

I'm glad Belz knows I'm missing and with this psycho, but I'm still not going to just sit around waiting for them to save me.

"If I were you, I'd get the idea of anyone coming to save you out of your head. See this?" He holds up a chain similar to Mom's with the same blue stone. "This prevents other demons from finding me. A gift from your lovely aunt after I told her I had a run-in with another demon. It also prevents any summons from reaching the intended demon while I'm around, so don't count on being able to summon anyone," he finishes with a smirk.

Well, fuck. Good thing I'm not planning on waiting for someone else to save me.

"I'll let you get comfortable. I'll be back when your aunt gets here," he tells me with a Cheshire grin, before backing out of the room and leaving me alone.

Yes, I can't wait to meet this witch. What kind of *family* does this? Have a repulsive demon kidnap her niece. What purpose does this serve? What is she getting out of this? The answers can't come soon enough.

TWENTY

MADELYNE

After Chad leaves, I search the room. The first thing I do is check the windows because obviously, I want out of this hell hole and that'd be my best bet. Unfortunately for me, they are completely sealed shut. Trust me, I tried. My fucking hands and arms hurt from pulling so much. They won't budge. So I go about trying to find some kind of weapon. As if whatever sorry excuse for a weapon I could find in this room is going to be any good against a couple of demons.

Not finding anything remotely useful, I plop down on the bed and try to think of the best strategy for getting out of here unharmed. Chad says the bitch that's helping him is my *aunt*. I don't have any family on my dad's side, so she must be my mom's sister. I can't recall dad ever talking about Mom's family. Which is really odd because growing up, he would tell me stories about her. I know as much about my mom as my dad does. So why didn't he know anything about her family? What was she hiding? The biggest question is, why would her sister want to hurt me?

Some time later, I'm not sure how long as I've been lost in thought, the door creaks open. I snap my head up to see Chad standing there looking like his every dream is about to come true.

"Come on, sweetie, time to meet your aunt. We've got big news to share with you." He smiles this maniacal grin that kinda creeps me out.

Not wanting him to put his nasty hands on me again, I stand and go willingly. I want to meet this bitch. See what kind of woman would turn on her family like this.

"Oh, good, you're finally coming around. I knew eventually you'd see reason. We were always going to be together, Maddy. It's about time you accept that."

He backs up as I get to the door, holding out an arm directing me back to the living room. Walking into the room, I stop dead in my tracks when I see the woman standing there. *What? It can't be. What is* she *doing here? Why?*

"Hello, daughter," Marjorie says. "Surprised to see me?"

Well, yeah. Why on earth would I suspect my fucking

step-mom of being my mom's sister with some sinister plan that has yet to be revealed to me. Since I don't actually answer her, just give her a weird look that I know drives her crazy, she continues with her evil villain speech.

"Your mother took everything from me, and now I'm going to take everything from her. First, let me fill you in on Mommy Dearest's dark secrets. You see, she didn't just up and leave you when you were a baby. She went back to Hell where she belongs."

The surprise must show on my face because she cackles in glee.

"That's right, your precious mommy who you've missed so much is a demon. But not just any demon. No, no. She's the favored daughter of the king of Hell himself. *I* should be the favored daughter! That stupid brat has done nothing to earn that role. Yet, no matter what I do, he just won't pay attention to me. Well, everyone will pay attention to me now," she whines, before continuing.

"It took me a long time to find out about your existence. Zofina refused to talk to *anyone* about her time on earth. I don't even remember how I stumbled on the information linking her to your father. I watched him for months, getting to know everything about his life before I finally introduced myself. He was so easy to manipulate... to a certain point. I could make him do whatever I wanted him to, except for when it came to *you*. He told me all about your mother and I convinced him you needed a mother figure. But you were immune to my charms. None of my powers worked on you. You must have gotten some of your mother's abilities. That's one of the things that incenses me the most about her. She's always been insusceptible to me. But I found my ways to control you regardless," she says with an evil laugh.

"And now it's finally time to take that control to the ultimate level. You see, when your mother left you, she left you unprotected, the fool. According to Hell law, any royal can perform a binding ceremony. This ceremony will tether you to the other demon for the rest of eternity. There is no escaping it. Not even Lucifer himself can undo a binding legally done by another of the royal line. And the demon you're bound to for all time has access to all of your powers," she explains with a smug smile.

"That's nice and all, but I don't *have* any powers." I roll my eyes at her.

"Imbecile!" she screeches, then backhands me across my face. "Of course you have powers you fucking *nitwit.* You think I would have wasted all of this time for *nothing?* Just before the prodigal daughter returned home, I was snooping in Father's library when I found something that put this whole plan into motion. A scroll with a prophecy from Remiel. Now since I know you never paid attention at church, I'll tell you, Remiel is an archangel responsible for divine visions. His visions are never wrong and he has never been known to have one concerning Hell or demons. However, this scroll said otherwise.

"Remiel sent my father the scroll telling him of a

vision he had of his granddaughter. He claimed Lucifer's favored daughter would find her fated mate in the unlikeliest of places and she would birth a daughter. This granddaughter was to be Lucifer's replacement when it finally came time for him to step down. She would be more powerful than the entire royal line *combined*. She would grow so powerful she could destroy Hell's empire completely or strengthen its dominion to levels even Lucifer couldn't achieve. She could tear the whole establishment to the ground, or she could bring all of Hell together. Spoiler, *you're* the granddaughter, and I plan on using you to burn the whole thing to the ground."

"Okay, so just to make sure I understand. You're going to bind me to fuckface here..." I hike a thumb in Chad's direction. "He's going to have access to these awesome powers I supposedly have, then you're going to use those powers to destroy Hell. Who's to say he's not going to take my powers for himself and use them against *you*? Are you sure you've thought this through?"

I can tell she's losing her patience with me but it just doesn't sound like a good plan.

"He would *never* betray me like that because he *loves* me, you cretin!" she screeches.

"That's right, baby," Chad purrs and it makes me want to gag. Then he walks up to her and they start making out. I think I just might vomit.

"Ugh. Gross. Get a room. Far away from me." I shudder in disgust. "You're doing all this because your daddy didn't love you enough? Aren't you a little old to have a temper tantrum of this magnitude?" I taunt. I'm sure it's not a good idea to provoke a crazy person, but I *need* them to stop kissing. Ewww.

My distraction tactic works because she snaps her head up and glares at me. If looks could kill, I swear her whole plan would be up in smoke right now because I'd be dead.

"It's not a tantrum you simpleton! It's *revenge*! And it will be mine!" she shrieks.

"Okay, okay. Have your revenge. Whatever," I snark with my hands raised in mock surrender.

"You think this is a game? Your life as you know it is over. You will be my prisoner for the rest of time. Not even the rest of your life. Once I drag you to Hell, you'll turn into the demon you were meant to be. You will live forever, locked up to be used however I see fit. There is no happily ever after for you, Madelyne," she sneers.

"What makes you think this will actually work? If I'm sooo powerful, why wouldn't I just destroy *you*?"

"Because you don't have access to your powers yet," she says smugly. Mother fucker. "And I'm going to bind you to Ugch'radd..." she starts but I cut her off.

"Wait... His name is... Ugch'radd?" I sputter. "Oh God, that's too much." I chuckle, wiping a tear from my eye.

Marjorie narrows her eyes at me before continuing. "As I was saying. I'm going to bind you to Ugch'radd."

Cue sputtering laughter again. I can tell she's getting

pissed that I keep interrupting her little speech, but oh my God. That's his *name?* Jesus, no wonder he goes by Chad. I wonder if he has all the demons call him Chad too. I know I would. She grinds her teeth together and her eyes start to go black like Belz's.

"You will be bound before you have access to your powers. *Then* when I take you to Hell you will get your powers, but by then it will be too late because you will already be under my control."

"Well, shit. I don't think I like this plan. Can we come up with another one? Maybe one that doesn't include me shackled to ugly McUglyson here? Besides, I think my real mates might have a problem with that. They only like to share with each other, ya know," I inform her with a wink.

"Mate? What mate?" she squeals, then turns to Chad. "You didn't tell me there were any other demons in the picture! Are you completely incompetent? If they've already mated, they'll find her here! We must hurry and do the ceremony now before it's too late. Take her to the basement and get her ready," she commands.

Shit, maybe that was the wrong thing to say. I've always had a problem keeping my mouth shut. I invariably say the wrong things at the wrong time. Chad's hands close around my biceps and he drags me to the stairs then down to a dingy basement. There's a table set up with candles and some kind of knife. I don't know, it doesn't look like a fun time to me. He shoves me into a chair and starts tying me up with rope. Fuck, this doesn't look good for me.

"Do you really think this is going to end well for you? What, you think as soon as I pop into Hell I'm going to instantly have all of the power and I'll overthrow fucking *Lucifer?* Don't you read? Shit's never that easy. It takes *time* to gain your power, to be strong enough to defeat the big bad. Not that I'd classify my grandfather as the big bad, but apparently you do," I say with a shrug. Well as much as I can shrug in my current state.

"You really need to learn when to shut up. It's over, Maddy. You lose, just accept it."

"Is she ready?" Marjorie calls down the stairs.

"She's secure. You can come down," Chad hollers back. "Let the fun begin." He chuckles at my murderous glare.

I hear the tell-tale sound of heels clicking on the stairs then Marjorie appears with a broad smile on her face. She spares me a glance on her way to the table where she lights the candles.

"Now, I could lie to you and tell you this won't hurt, but… It will. It will be excruciating. Especially if you already have mate bonds. It will feel like your very soul is being torn apart. Because… well it *is.* You see before I can bind you to him, I have to unbind you from your mate. It won't be a fun experience. For you that is. I'll get a lot of enjoyment from watching you suffer. Chad, darling, be a dear and hold her still will you?"

Oh hell no. That is *not* fucking happening. They want to threaten *me*, they can do that all they want. But I will *not* let them take my mates from me. As Chad approaches me, I feel my entire body start to heat. It feels like I'm on fire by the time he reaches me. As soon as he puts his hands on me, he screams in agony, backing away with them raised. I can see red blisters already oozing covering both hands. I feel the rope go slack and look down to see it's burnt to a crisp. It's literally ashes in my lap.

Marjorie turns at his screams and I jump up from my seat with a sinister smile on my face. These fuckers thought they could do whatever they wanted to me? Oh no, sweetie. You got the wrong bitch. I slowly stalk towards my wicked stepmother, my smile reminiscent of the Joker's.

"Chad! What are you doing? Stop her!" She cries as she retreats, bumping her back into the wall.

Chad, the fucking idiot that he is, starts to approach me. I barely spare him a glance before I flick my hand out and he stops, surrounded by blue flames licking at his torso. Turning back to the problem at hand, I smirk at the bitch who thought to ruin my life.

"Don't think he's going to be much help, *Mommy Dearest*," I sneer.

She narrows her eyes and I catch the twitch of her hand in time to counter the fireball she sails at my head. These powers are completely new to me, but it feels so natural to flick my hand and send a wisp of smoke to wrap around her hands and pin her to the wall. Her eyes widen as she realizes she's trapped and at my mercy. Considering the things she just threatened to do to me, it's not a predicament she wants to be in.

I stand there, pondering what I should do next. I can't just let them go. Who's to say they won't come after me again? No, this has to end now. When I focus back on the woman that spent almost two decades pretending to care about me, her eyes are wider than I've ever seen, she's struggling in her bounds against the wall and ranting.

"No, no. Let me go, please. I'll leave you alone. You'll never see me again. Please don't take me to him. I'm sorry, I'm sorry."

"The time for apologies is long over, sister. I see my daughter has things under control though, so I'm just here for backup," a sugary sweet voice calls from behind me.

I spin around and come face to face with the most beautiful woman I've ever seen. She hasn't changed a bit. She looks exactly like she did in the picture I was just looking at earlier tonight. Must be a demon thing. I should say something, but I just stand there staring. I've dreamed of the day I would see my mom again, but I can honestly say it never went down like this.

"Madelyne. You're every bit as beautiful as Belzar said you were," she says in a reverent voice.

"Mom? Is it… Is it really you?" I ask hesitantly. I'm afraid this is all some trick. Just a mind game Majorie is playing on me to break me.

"It's me, sweet girl."

Just then I hear a commotion as feet bound down the stairs.

"Zofina! I swear to the devil himself..." Belz trails off as he finally reaches the basement and sees me. "*Amica Mea*! Oh, thank the heavens!" He runs over to me, wrapping me in his strong embrace and holding me so tight my back cracks.

"Easy there, big guy. I'm fine. Put me down." I groan as I pat his shoulder.

He reluctantly releases me and takes a step back, hands still on my shoulders. "You're okay? They didn't hurt you?"

"Not at all. They didn't make it that far. See the bitch attached to the wall?" I ask. At his nod and a chorus of "mmhmms" from the other guys I hadn't noticed, I continue. "Well, *that's* Marjorie. My stepmother," I declare.

"Stepmother?" My mom, Zofina I guess, snarls as she steps next to me. "That's where you've been? Living *my* life? Why you little..." She marches right up to her and punches her in the face so hard her head snaps to the side, slamming into the wall. "Oh, I'm going to have fun torturing you."

She turns her back on her and walks back to me. "Madelyne. I'm so sorry. I never should have left you."

"I'm sure you had a good reason. Dad always said you wouldn't have left us unless it was absolutely necessary. He never mentioned you were a demon though."

She has the decency to look chagrined. "I never told him. I was trying to keep him safe. Both of you. I didn't want demons and Hell to be a part of your life. I wanted you to live a happy clueless life. You were so sweet and innocent. I couldn't take that away from you. I see now I was wrong. I made so many bad decisions that could have been completely avoided had I just stopped and *talked*. But I was scared. I didn't want to lose your father. I thought he would think I was crazy, try to have me committed. I was so stupid. I wish I would have done things differently. I wish I didn't miss out on your whole life because I was too stupid to tell my father what was going on with me. He wants to meet you, by the way, both of you."

"Umm, yeah. That's a lot to take in right now. Can we maybe get together and hash this out? Because I would love to have you in my life, but it's going to take more than just popping in saying you're sorry and everything's good, we're a happy family now. But fuck. I don't guess I have much of a choice when it comes to meeting the fucking devil, do I?"

"Don't think of him as the devil. He's your grandfather. He's sad that he's missed out on being a part of your life," she assures me.

Belz squeezes my waist and I look up into his loving eyes. "Maybe later. Right now, I want to take my mates home. It's been a long stressful day," I announce, looking around for Zeph and finding two of him and another devilishly handsome demon. Jesus, how are they all so fucking hot?

One of the Zephyrs steps forward with a sinful smile on his face. "Yes, I think you deserve some downtime. Let us take care of you, baby."

Tall, dark, and handsome in the back coughs awkwardly. "Right, well, I'm just gonna go home now. Looks like you've got this all handled. Zo, want me to take one of these fuckers to the cells?" he offers.

"Thank you, Oz. You can take him. Make sure he makes it alive," she orders with an arched brow.

"Ugh. You're no fun." At her narrowed eyes he sighs. "Fine, he'll get there *alive*. That's the only guarantee you'll get. Madelyne, it was a pleasure meeting you. Nice to see you're not some damsel in distress that depends on a man to save you," he snarks, then snaps his fingers, and Chad is gone, Oz following after.

"That's so cool! Can you do that? Can *I* do that?" I ask the room, getting a round of laughter in return. What? I'm serious. I want to snap my fingers and disappear. That would be badass.

"Come here, love, I'll show you what I can do." Zephyr winks at me, holding out a hand for me to take, which I do.

He pulls me into his chest and claims my lips in a desperate kiss. I can feel the dread and uneasiness rolling off his body. Wrapping my arms around his head, I smother those doubts and fear with my love, kissing him as if I would die if I didn't. I hear someone coughing again and someone saying "That's enough, you two," but I pay no mind to them. I need this. Zephyr needs this. Next thing I know, I feel wisps of smoke surrounding us like we're inside a tornado. When the smoke clears, we're in my bedroom.

"Oh look at that! I *can* do that too," I giggle as I look around the room.

TWENTY-ONE

ZEPHYR

"**H**ow did you? You know what, I don't care. Fuck, I was so worried, Maddy." I pull her back into my arms. I never want to let go of her. I swear, she's not leaving my sight for a long while after this.

"Hey! I was worried too, you know? I had no way of summoning you. I couldn't get ahold of Belz… Shit, Belz!" She pulls back from me with a gasp then flings her hand toward the bed beside us.

Next thing I know there's a cloud of smoke covering the bed and when it clears there's a pissed-off Belz.

"Oops?" She smiles with a little shrug.

"Oops? Don't think just because you have powers now that I won't tan that hide," he threatens.

She must like the idea though because she just wiggles her brows at him in return. "Promise?"

His nostrils flare and he sits up on the bed, crawling over to us. "You better believe it, *Amica Mea.*" He reaches out, grabbing her and pulling her down on the bed with him as she squeals with laughter.

"Not to ruin the moment or anything, but what happened with Zofina and Marjorkorie?"

"Mar-jor-korie?" Maddy sputters a laugh. "Oh my God, is that her name?" she asks as she falls into a peal of giggles.

"It is. And Zar escorted them to Hell. Seems Luc promised to have his torture chamber cleaned for their arrival. Kinda wish I could be a fly on that wall."

"Shiiit. His own daughter? Not that she doesn't deserve everything that's coming to her and more. But damn."

"Can we worry about them later? I believe someone promised to take care of me," Maddy smirks from the bed and I have to agree, everything else can wait.

Belz and I are on the same page because he turns and starts kissing her as I climb up the bed. They're pretty hot and heavy by the time I reach them and I love the sounds coming from them. Reaching between them, I grab the waistband of her pants and pull them down her thighs. She kicks her legs and sends the offending material flying to the edge of the bed.

Chuckling, I kiss up her ankles, loving the sweet, intoxicating scent on her smooth skin. She smells good enough to eat, and I plan on doing just that. I press my lips to her heated core over her panties before working my way up. Biting the waistband, I pull them down with my teeth, as she moans and lifts her ass to help me. Once they're off and join the pants, I look up her thick, curvy body and watch Belz remove her shirt revealing her flushed bare chest. I squeeze her thighs as I watch Belz cup one breast, lift it and twirl his tongue around her hard nipple.

"You're so fucking sexy, Maddy. I could watch him torment your tits all day, but I think I'll amplify your torment instead," I growl, before diving down and swiping my tongue up her slit.

One fucking taste of her tangy nectar and I'm done for. I burrow my tongue deep in her pussy, licking her walls. A thrill runs through me as she grabs my hair and holds my face to her. *That's right baby, take what you want from me. I would gladly drown in your juices.* Squeezing her legs, I pin them to the bed as I devour her pussy.

"Oh, fuck! Please, I need more," she gasps between moans.

Never one to deny her, I swap my tongue for my fingers, stretching her hot pussy, as I add two, then three. Curling my fingers up, I rub her G-spot as I gently lick her clit, timing my swipes to her groans. The more she moans, the faster I lick. It's a good thing my tongue is so dexterous because her moans are constant. Once her pussy starts gripping my fingers so tight I know it's only a matter of seconds before she explodes, I pull them from her and press a gentle kiss on her mound.

At my abrupt stop, she shoves Belz off of her and glares down at me. "What the fuck are you doing? Why the hell did you stop? I was about to come!"

"I know. That's why I stopped."

I swear if looks could kill... well, they *can,* so thank fuck she doesn't know about that yet, otherwise, I'd be a dead demon.

"What's the matter, Angel, never heard of delayed gratification? Just think how good it'll be when you finally get that orgasm you want so badly."

"Belz, you'll give me an orgasm won't you?" she pouts.

"I don't know, *Amica Mea,* I think he's right. Could be fun to see you go completely crazy for us," he tells her.

"Be careful what you wish for. You may get the wrong kind of crazy. Now, I think you two have too much clothing on." She smirks before she snaps her fingers and our clothes turn to ash. "Oh, yeah. I'm gonna like this power," she cackles.

I never thought I'd find a cackle sexy, but here we are. Belz, being the one lying beside her, grabs her by the hips and twists, rolling over and pulling her on top of him. Adjusting herself, she sits up to straddle him, rubbing her wet pussy all over his cock as she does.

"Woman," he growls. "Stay still." He squeezes her waist and stops her from squirming.

Once she gives in and stops moving, he picks her up and turns to me. "A little help?"

Licking my lips, I crawl over and wrap my hand around his throbbing dick, stroking it once, twice, before pointing it at Maddy's waiting pussy. I rub the head through her slick folds and she groans before Belz pulls her down on it.

"Oooooh yesss. Mm-more," she begs as she rocks her hips forward, seeking more friction.

I pull my hand out from between them and Belz slams her down causing her to scream at the unexpected fullness. Not wanting to be left out, I skim my hands up her soft sides, loving the shiver that runs through her body at my touch. Kneeling behind her, I press my chest to her back as I smooth my hands across her supple stomach and up to her full breasts, cupping each of them in my hands. Giving them a firm squeeze, I run my nose up her neck, nipping at her delicate skin as I moan in her ear.

"Oh, God! Yes. Fuck, I love it when you work together," she moans as she grinds down on Belz.

"That's it, baby, squeeze me hard. Mmmm. You like riding my cock while Zeph fondles those luscious tits, don't you? Oh, yeah. That twitch says you do. Pinch her nipples, Z."

I do as I'm told, pinching both nipples hard, loving the scream that falls from her lips.

"Oooooh, yes!" She slams her hands down on Belz's chest and sits up on her knees, pulling herself off of him only to slam back down. She does this over and over while chanting "Yes, yes, yes."

I'm about to remove my hands because she's getting too close, but she covers them with her own. Holding them to her chest as she fucks Belz, her moans getting louder and louder.

"Oh, God! Fuck me, Belz, fuck me!" she screams and it seems he can't hold out any longer because he puts his feet flat on the bed and thrusts up into her. "Yes! God, yes! Just like that! Fuck, don't stop! Don't you ever fucking stop!" she cries as he continues pounding into her and she twists her hips so his cock hits her in just the right place.

Wanting to be a more active participant, I lick, kiss, suck her neck, and behind her ear, sucking it into my mouth, pulling it with my teeth as she screams her release.

She lets go of my hands and collapses on top of Belz. I kiss my way up her spine, moving up the bed as I go. When I get to her head, I kiss the crown then lean down and kiss Belz.

"Good job," I tell him with a grin before lying down beside them.

"Give me ten minutes, then we can have round two. Zeph, be ready," she grumbles into Belz's chest.

"You got it, hot stuff. Ten minutes and you're mine," I agree, knowing full well she's about to pass the fuck out.

Belz and I share a knowing look as she closes her eyes. I don't mind. I can wait. We've got the rest of our lives to explore each other's bodies.

TWENTY-TWO

MADELYNE

"So what exactly does it mean to be Lucifer's granddaughter? Do you know anything about this prophecy Marjorie was going on about?" I ask Belz the next morning. It was great reuniting with my guys, but some serious shit went down last night and I need answers. Is Marjorie just a nutcase or was she telling the truth?

"I do not, but I'm sure Luc will explain everything when he meets you. Don't worry so much, *Amica Mea,*" he assures me with a kiss on the forehead, as he walks by to make his second cup of coffee.

"And *how* am I going to meet the devil? He can't leave Hell, right? That's gonna make it a little hard, don't ya think?" I cross my arms and roll my eyes at the idea.

"Ummm... you'll go... to Hell? You're a demon, Maddy. You can go to Hell," Zeph hesitantly explains like it should have been obvious.

"Huh. Guess I haven't thought about that implication. I got so caught up on the whole 'Mom is a princess of Hell' and 'Granddad is the freaking *devil'*, I didn't stop to think about what that really meant. Soooo. I'm a demon. Does that mean I have to live in Hell? I have a life here. I can't just up and leave, ya know," I ramble as I start pacing my living room.

"I don't know, Angel. I do know Luc is going to want to meet you. Soon. We won't know any of the answers to your questions until you go to Gehenna. Now come sit with me. You're going to wear a hole in the carpet." Zeph holds out his hand, with his brows raised.

Pausing my pacing, I heave a sigh. He's right. I'm just stressing myself out thinking about all the what-ifs. I won't know anything until I ask the right person. Dragging my feet to the chair Zeph is sitting in, my favorite comfy chair, of course, I plop down on his lap, wrapping my arms around his neck and laying my head down on his shoulder. His arms instantly go around my back holding me close. I think yesterday was really tough on him. He hasn't let me out of his sight, going so far as to follow me to the bathroom. It's sweet, but I don't know how much more I can take. I think I proved last night that I can handle myself.

"What's Gehenna?" I ask into his neck.

"It's the capital city of Hell. It's where we live, where the castle is," he explains.

"How are we going to get there?"

"I'm going to take you, Daughter."

I jump at the unexpected voice and Zeph's arms squeeze tighter, silently reassuring me it's okay.

"How do you do that? The guys have to be summoned, but you seem to be able to just pop in wherever you want."

"The perks of being royal, my dear. You'll be able to do it too when you learn how to use all of your powers."

Well, that's cool. I wonder what other powers I'll get.

"Come, come. Father is only so patient. I told him you needed your rest after the ordeal last night, but we shouldn't keep him waiting long. Up. Get dressed. Surely you have something more presentable than that," she giggles at my pajamas.

The pants have little pitchforks and flames all over them and the tank top has a red devil character and it says 'I'm the devil'. Reed got them for me for Christmas one year. It was his fuck you to my stepmom and her churchy ways. If only he knew.

"I don't know, you don't think this is the perfect outfit to meet the devil in?" I joke.

Belz walks back into the room, sipping his coffee. Bringing his mug down he smiles. "I think Luc would get a kick out of it. I vote you wear it," he chuckles.

"It's settled! If Gramps wants to meet me, he should

meet the real me, not the polite me Marjorie tried to mold me into," I declare as I hop off Zeph's lap.

"He's going to love you just like I do," Mom—I'm still not used to that, but I figure the more I refer to her that way, the more natural it'll feel—assures me. "Okay, hold my hand and I'll bring you to him. Boys, we're going to Father's office. I take it, you'll meet us there?"

"Of course," they answer in unison.

Shaking my head at their overprotective antics, I take Mom's outstretched hand and marvel at the wisps of smoke surrounding us.

The smoke clears to reveal a stately office with dark mahogany shelves built into the walls. They're filled with books and knick-knacks, and I'd love to take a closer look, but I don't want to be caught snooping. A matching desk with intricately carved legs that end in claw feet, takes up a quarter of the room. There's a massive black wingback chair sitting behind the desk, which oddly enough, has a *computer* on it! *They have computers in Hell?*

Turning, I see there's a couch that matches the chair on the other side of the room. There's a coffee table that looks like a miniature version of the desk, and a tall lamp standing in the corner. It looks nothing like what I would expect the devil's office to look like. Honestly, it's rather homey. It has a welcoming feel to it that I can't understand. You would think he would put off an air of 'stay the fuck away from me', but I'm not getting that from this room.

A hand on my back startles me out of my wandering thoughts.

"You okay, *Amica Mea?*" Belz whispers.

I turn into his arms and look up at him with a smile. "I'm fine. Was just checking out the room. It's not what I was expecting at all. It looks like something I'd see on Earth. Granted in an outrageously expensive house, but still."

"Does that mean you approve of my decorating tastes, Granddaughter?" A smooth voice calls from behind Belz.

Oh, God. It's time. I'm meeting the devil. Shit. Probably shouldn't say God around the devil. Instead of giving an intelligent answer, I squeak. That's right. My reaction to the devil talking to me is to squeak like a damn mouse. *This is my life ladies and gentlemen.*

The devil, of course, *snickers*. "Move, Belzar, I want to meet my granddaughter."

Belz, the kind soul that he is, looks to me for... reassurance? Permission? I don't know, but it's sweet that he took the time to check in with me, to make sure I was okay before he obeyed the fucking *devil*. He's got balls, my demon. I smile up at him and bounce on my toes to kiss him in thanks before stepping to the side.

"Well, shit. Looks like all those books I read were

right. The devil *is* hot. That's not creepy at all considering you're my grandfather," I ramble.

The room fills with laughter and I smack myself for my lack of filter.

"Madelyne. It is a pleasure to meet you. You are just like your mother," he chuckles. "We're going to get along marvelously. Love the pjs. Though you're not the devil *yet*," he adds with a wink.

"Please, sit, sit," he instructs before snapping his fingers, a cloud of swirling black smoke appearing and dissolving almost immediately to reveal a comfy-looking seat that he gracefully sits in. "Sooo, how was your childhood? Did you have friends? Were you happy? Do you like dogs? I have a dog. Oh! What's your favorite color?" he rushes through question after question, I swear he doesn't even pause to breathe and his excitement just amps up more and more with each one.

"Wow. You're excited, huh?" I chuckle.

"Oh, sorry. Yes, I'm very excited. I just want to know everything about you. So, start from the beginning. Don't skip the boring parts."

"Father. She can't tell you every detail of her life," Mom chastises him.

"Well, why not? I want to know," he pouts. Yes, the fucking *devil* is pouting over *me*. "She's my only grandchild, I think I have the right to know every detail of her life," he sulks.

"I would love to tell you every detail, but

unfortunately, my memory just isn't that good," I offer with a shrug. "I can give you a quick rundown though?"

"Why does it have to be quick? We have all the time in the world," he grumbles.

"Actually, I uhh… I have work?"

He furrows his brows and turns to my mother, then my mates, finally stopping on me. "You… knooow… you're not… um. I'm sorry to be the one to tell you this, Madelyne, but you have to stay here. We have much to discuss. It can't be rushed."

"What do you mean I have to *stay* here? I can't stay here." I shake my head adamantly, looking around the room waiting for someone to tell me 'the devil is crazy, don't listen to him'. But no, instead I get a mix of 'yay, you're staying!' and 'sorry I didn't warn you' looks. Well, *fuck*.

TO CONTINUE ON...

Find out what happens when Maddy gets stuck in hell in the next installment of Madelyne Danica.
Coming soon.

ABOUT SCARLETT PHILIPS

Let's see… I'm a 33 y/o mother of 4. Three girls, ages 12, 7, & 5, and a boy also 5. Yes, I have twins. Lol The youngest 3 all have autism, so I spend my days driving them back and forth to therapy. About 4 years ago, I decided I needed a hobby. Other than mindlessly watching tv. So I started reading, and haven't stopped, also haven't really watched tv since. lol My longest weekly streak on Kindle was 122 weeks. Sadly, I broke my streak when I started writing and took a break from reading. I know some of you will understand the heartbreak. I write books that combine the real world with fantasy, currently, that's in the form of a magical small-town reverse harem.

ALSO BY SCARLETT PHILIPS

Everton Ever After

Returning to Everton - books2read.com/everton1

Surviving in Everton - books2read.com/everton2

Dating in Everton - books2read.com/everton3

Returning to Everton Duet (omnibus) -
books2read.com/evertonduet1

Co-write with Iris James: Saving Supetopia Series

Not Again! - books2read.com/notagain

Saving Supetopia Book Two - https://books2read.com/u/3yaOjl

Madelyne Danica

How to Accidentally Summon a Demon -
books2read.com/htasad

Printed in Great Britain
by Amazon